William Shakespeare's Othello: A Retelling in Prose

David Bruce

Published by David Bruce, 2022.

WILLIAM SHAKESPEARE'S OTHELLO: A RETELLING IN PROSE

First edition. July 28, 2022.

Copyright © 2022 David Bruce.

ISBN: 979-8201469238

Written by David Bruce.

Table of Contents

Dedication

Dedicated to Carl Eugene Bruce and Josephine Saturday Bruce

My father, Carl Eugene Bruce, died on 24 October 2013. He used to work for Ohio Power, and at one time, his job was to shut off the electricity of people who had not paid their bills. He sometimes would find a home with an impoverished mother and some children. Instead of shutting off their electricity, he would tell the mother that she needed to pay her bill or soon her electricity would be shut off. He would write on a form that no one was home when he stopped by because if no one was home he did not have to shut off their electricity.

The best good deed that anyone ever did for my father occurred after a storm that knocked down many power lines. He and other linemen worked long hours and got wet and cold. Their feet were freezing because water got into their boots and soaked their socks. Fortunately, a kind woman gave my father and the other linemen dry socks to wear.

My mother, Josephine Saturday Bruce, died on 14 June 2003. She used to work at a store that sold clothing. One day, an impoverished mother with a baby clothed in rags walked into the store and started shoplifting in an interesting way: The mother took the rags off her baby and dressed the infant in new clothing. My mother knew that this mother could not afford to buy the clothing, but she helped the mother dress her baby and then she watched as the mother walked out of the store without paying.

***

The doing of good deeds is important. As a free person, you can choose to live your life as a good person or as a bad person. To be a good person, do good deeds. To be a bad person, do bad deeds. If you do good deeds, you will become good. If you do bad deeds, you will become bad. To become the person you want to be, act as if you already are that kind of person. Each of us chooses what kind of person we will become. To become a good person, do the things a good person does. To become a bad person, do the things a bad person does. The opportunity to take action to become the kind of person you want to be is yours.

Human beings have free will. According to the Babylonian Niddah 16b, whenever a baby is to be conceived, the Lailah (angel in charge of contraception) takes the drop of semen that will result in the conception and asks God, "Sovereign of the Universe, what is going to be the fate of this drop? Will it develop into a robust or into a weak person? An intelligent or a stupid person? A wealthy or a poor person?" The Lailah asks all these questions, but it does not ask, "Will it develop into a righteous or a wicked person?" The answer to that question lies in the decisions to be freely made by the human being that is the result of the conception.

A Buddhist monk visiting a class wrote this on the chalkboard: "EVERYONE WANTS TO SAVE THE WORLD, BUT NO ONE WANTS TO HELP MOM DO THE DISHES." The students laughed, but the monk then said, "Statistically, it's highly unlikely that any of you will ever have the opportunity to run into a burning orphanage and rescue an infant. But, in the smallest gesture of kindness — a warm smile, holding the door for the person behind you, shoveling the driveway of the elderly person next door — you have committed an act of immeasurable profundity, because to each of us, our life is our universe."

In her book titled *I Have Chosen to Stay and Fight*, comedian Margaret Cho writes, "I believe that we get complimentary snack-size portions of the afterlife, and we all receive them in a different way." For Ms. Cho, many of her snack-size portions of the afterlife come in hip hop music. Other people get different snack-size portions of the afterlife, and we all must be on the lookout for them when they come our way. And perhaps doing good deeds and experiencing good deeds are snack-size portions of the afterlife.

The Zen master Gisan was taking a bath. The water was too hot, so he asked a student to add some cold water to the bath. The student brought a bucket of cold water, added some cold water to the bath, and then threw the rest of the water on a rocky path. Gisan scolded the student: "Everything can be used. Why did you waste the rest of the water by pouring it on the path? There are some plants nearby which could have used the water. What right do you have to waste even a drop of water?" The student became enlightened and changed his name to Tekisui, which means "Drop of Water."

Educate Yourself
Read Like A Wolf Eats
Be Excellent to Each Other
Books Then, Books Now, Books Forever

***

In this retelling, as in all my retellings, I have tried to make the work of literature accessible to modern readers who may lack some of the knowledge about mythology, religion, and history that the literary work's contemporary audience had.

Do you know a language other than English? If you do, I give you permission to translate this book, copyright your translation, publish or self-publish it, and keep all the royalties for yourself. (Do give me credit, of course, for the original retelling.)

I would like to see my retellings of classic literature used in schools, so I give permission to the country of Finland (and all other countries) to give copies of this book to all students forever. I also give permission to the state of Texas (and all other states) to give copies of this book to all students forever. I also give permission to all teachers to give copies of this book to all students forever.

Teachers need not actually teach my retellings. Teachers are welcome to give students copies of my eBooks as background material. For example, if they are teaching Homer's *Iliad* and *Odyssey*, teachers are welcome to give students copies of my *Virgil's* Aeneid: *A Retelling in Prose* and tell students, "Here's another ancient epic you may want to read in your spare time.

CAST OF CHARACTERS

Male Characters

DUKE OF VENICE.

BRABANTIO, a Venetian senator, father to Desdemona.

GRATIANO, a noble Venetian and brother to Brabantio.

LODOVICO, a noble Venetian and kinsman to Brabantio.

OTHELLO, the Moor, in the military service of Venice.

CASSIO, an honorable lieutenant to Othello.

IAGO, an ensign, aka standard-bearer, aka ancient, to Othello; a villain.

RODERIGO, a Venetian gentleman.

MONTANO, governor of Cyprus, replaced by Othello.

Clown, servant to Othello.

Female Characters

DESDEMONA, wife to Othello.

EMILIA, wife to Iago.

BIANCA, a courtesan who is mistress to Cassio.

Other Characters

SENATORS, SAILORS, GENTLEMEN OF CYPRUS, OFFICERS, MESSENGERS, MUSICIANS.

CHAPTER 1
— 1.1 —

Late at night on a street in Venice, Italy, Iago and Roderigo were in the middle of a conversation.

Roderigo said, "Bah! Don't even try to make me believe that! I have trusted you, and I have let you spend my money as if it were your own. I can't believe what I am hearing!"

"You are not listening to me," Iago said. "I never dreamed that such a thing could happen. If I have, then hate me forever."

"You told me that you hate him."

"Indeed, I do," Iago replied. "Hate me if I do not hate him. Three VIPs of Venice went to him to ask him to make me his lieutenant. They removed their hats as they stood in front of him to show their respect for him. By the faith of humanity, I know my worth, and I know that I deserve to be his lieutenant. But he, being proud and wanting to make his own decision, ignored them. Instead, he came up with a bombastic reason stuffed with military jargon to ignore their request and said, "Assuredly, I have already chosen my lieutenant." And who was his new lieutenant? Indeed, he was a great theorist, a Florentine — a foreigner — named Michael Cassio, who is a dandy and ladies man who has avoided ruining his bachelor fun by avoiding marriage. He has no personal experience of warfare. He has never positioned a squadron in the field. He does not know how to methodically arrange troops on a battlefield any more than a spinster knows. All he knows is textbook theory; our inexperienced Venetian senators can talk as 'masterly' as he can. Cassio's soldiership is all talk and no experience, and all his talk is mere prattle. But he, sir, was chosen to be lieutenant, while I, whose worth has been witnessed in battles at Rhodes, Cyprus, and other places — both Christian places and heathen places in the crusading wars — have been stopped in my advancement. I am like a ship that is in the lee and becalmed — another ship stands between the wind and me and so keeps me from moving forward. This bookkeeper, this petty accountant, will be lieutenant, while I — God help me! — must continue to be his Moorship's ancient — his standard-bearer, his ensign."

Anyone in Venice hearing this conversation would realize that Iago and Roderigo were talking about Othello, a Moor — a black North African — who served Venice as a military commander. The word "Moorship" is a portmanteau term combining "Moor" and the respectful term "Worship," but Iago was not using the word "Moorship" respectfully. As standard-bearer, Iago carried the distinctive flag identifying his unit, but he wanted a promotion to lieutenant — a promotion that Othello had denied to him and given to Michael Cassio instead. This was one of the reasons why Iago hated Othello.

"By Heaven, I would prefer to be his executioner than his standard-bearer," Roderigo said.

"I know of no way to remedy this situation," Iago said. "This is the curse of military service. Advancement and promotions come about because of influence and favoritism, and not by seniority, where the person second in line would eventually take over from the first person. Now, sir, judge for yourself whether I in any just way am required to respect and serve and be loyal to the Moor."

"I would not follow him then," Roderigo said.

"Oh, sir, know that I follow him only in order to use him for my own advantage. We cannot all be masters, and not all masters will be loyally followed. We see many a duteous and bowing servant knave, who, enjoying his own obsequious bondage, wears out his life, much like his master's ass, for nothing but provender, and when he's old, he's cashiered — he's fired and left to forage for himself. Let such honest and respectable knaves be whipped.

"Others there are who, showing outwardly all forms and visages of duty, keep yet their hearts intent on helping themselves. They give their lords shows of service and thrive at their lords' expense. When they have stuffed their coats with money, they do themselves homage and praise themselves.

"These fellows have some spirit, and I consider myself to be such a fellow. For, sir, it is as sure as you are Roderigo that, were I the Moor, I would not be Iago — if I were the Moor, I would not be fooled by an Iago because I would see through him and realize that he was putting on a show of loyalty to me. In seeming to follow him, I follow only myself; I am loyal to only myself and I work only to profit myself. As Heaven is my judge, I do not serve him out of love and duty, but only seem to. Why? So that I may profit by so doing.

"Right now, I do not act openly as I would like to act. Eventually, I will do so. Right now, I will wear my false heart upon my sleeve the way that a servant wears a badge that shows which family he serves. My false heart will falsely say that I truly serve Othello.

"Later, my actions will match what I truly think and feel. Then, I will allow jackdaws — foolish people — to wise up and peck at my false heart and tear it away, revealing my true character to all. Everyone will then know that I am not what I seem to be. I will reverse the moral of the fable of the bird in borrowed feathers — in the fable, a jackdaw dresses in the feathers of a peacock, but once the peacocks know what the jackdaw is doing, they rip the borrowed feathers (and the jackdaw's own feathers) away from the jackdaw's body. The moral of that fable is to not dress in borrowed feathers, but my dressing in borrowed feathers will help me achieve my goals."

"The thick-lips will have a full fortune if he can get away with this elopement!" Roderigo said.

"Call to and wake up her father. Rouse him out of bed, pester him, poison his delight, proclaim his business in the streets, and incense her kinsmen. Even though her father dwells in a fertile climate, plague him with flies. Even though his joy is real joy, yet throw such changes of vexation on his joy that it may lose some color and joyfulness."

"Here is her father's house," Roderigo said. "I'll call to him."

"Do that," Iago said. "Call to him with such a frightening and dire yell as is used when a fire in a populous city is started by negligence at night."

"Brabantio, wake up! Signior Brabantio, get up!" Roderigo shouted.

"Wake up!" Iago shouted. "Brabantio! Thieves! Thieves! Thieves! Look after your house, your daughter, and your moneybags! Thieves! Thieves!"

Brabantio, a senator of Venice and the father of Desdemona, appeared at a second-story window and asked, "What is the reason for this terrible racket? What is the matter?"

Roderigo replied, "Signior, is all your family inside your house?"

Iago asked, "Are your doors locked?"

"Why are you asking me these questions?"

"Sir, you have been robbed," Iago said. "Get dressed. Your heart has burst, and you have lost half your soul. Even now, right now, an old black ram is tupping your white ewe. Arise! Arise! Awake the snoring citizens with the bell, or else the black devil will make a grandfather of you. Arise, I say."

"What, have you lost your wits?" Brabantio asked.

"Most reverend signior, do you know my voice?" Roderigo asked.

"No. Who are you?"

"My name is Roderigo."

"You are even less welcome now than you were before," Brabantio said. "I have ordered you not to loiter around my doors. In honest plainness you have heard me say that my daughter is not for you, no matter how much you think you love her, but now you — full of supper and maddening alcoholic draughts that fill you with malicious bravery — have come to disrupt my quiet life."

"Sir, sir, sir —" Roderigo started to speak.

Brabantio interrupted, "You will learn that my character and place as a senator of Venice give me the power to punish these actions of yours and make you regret them."

"Patience, good sir!" Roderigo said.

"Why are you two talking to me about my house being robbed? This is Venice. My home is not an isolated house in the countryside."

"Most grave and respected Brabantio, with sincere and disinterested motivation I come to you," Roderigo lied.

Iago said to Brabantio, "Damn, sir, you are one of those people who will not serve God even when the devil — who is black — orders you to. You will not take good advice when it comes from a person whom you dislike. Although we come to do you good, you ignore us because you think we are ruffians. Because of that, you'll have your daughter covered sexually by a Barbary stallion. By Barbary, I mean Arabian, and by Arabian, I mean Moorish. Your grandchildren will neigh to you; you will have racehorses for kin and small Spanish horses for your blood relations."

Brabantio, who did not recognize Iago's voice, asked, "What profane wretch are you?"

"I am one, sir, who comes to tell you that your daughter and the Moor are now making the beast with two backs — they are having sex."

"You are a villain."

"You are —" Iago thought about using a cruelly insulting term, but instead finished his sentence with "— a senator."

"You will have to pay for tonight's outrage! I know your identity, Roderigo!"

"Sir, I will pay whatever you think I owe you," Roderigo said. "If it be your pleasure and you have given most wise consent that your beautiful daughter, just after midnight this night, be transported, with no worse nor better guard than a knave of common hire, a gondolier, and given to the gross clasps of a lascivious Moor — if this is known to you and you have given your permission to your daughter to marry the Moor, as I partly suspect to be the case, judging by your words to us — then we have done you bold and insolent wrongs. But if you do not know what your daughter has done, my code of conduct tells me that you have wrongly rebuked us. Do not believe that I, contrary to all sense of civility, would play and trifle with the respect that is due to you. Your daughter, if you have not given her permission to marry the Moor, has made a disgusting revolt against your wishes. She has tied her duty, beauty, intelligence, and fortunes to an extravagant and wheeling stranger who wanders widely here and everywhere. Immediately look and see whether your daughter is in her bedchamber or elsewhere in your house. If she is, then let us suffer the state's punishment for lying to and upsetting you."

Finally convinced that perhaps Roderigo was telling the truth when he said that his daughter was no longer in his house, Brabantio called out to his servants, "Strike a spark on the tinder! Give me a candle! Wake up all my relatives! This report by Roderigo is not unlike my dream. Belief in it oppresses me already. Light, I say! Bring me light!"

He disappeared from the second-story window.

Iago said to Roderigo, "Farewell; I must leave you. It is not wise — if I want to keep my job — for me to be made to give evidence against the Moor, as I will have to if I stay and am found here. The police will make me talk. What we have done may gall the Moor and cause him a little trouble, but it will do him no serious harm. He will not be fired from his position of military leader because he is needed to defend the island of Cyprus and keep Venice safe. Venice's war against the Turks is ongoing, and the Moor's competence makes him the right choice to be a military leader. To save their lives, the Venetian senators can find no one with the Moor's competence and experience to lead their military forces. Although I hate the Moor as much as I do the torments of Hell, yet because it is necessary to keep my job, I must pretend to respect him and put on a good show. You will find the Moor with me at the Sagittary Inn. Lead Brabantio and the men he wakes up there. Farewell."

Iago left, and Brabantio and some servants carrying torches came out of his house.

"It is too true an evil," Brabantio said. "My daughter is gone. The rest of my despised life will be spent in bitterness. Now, Roderigo, where did you see her? Oh, unhappy girl! She is with the Moor, did you say? Having experienced this, I have to ask why anyone would want to be a father! How did you know it was she? She has deceived me past all comprehension! What did she say to you?"

He ordered his servants, "Get more candles and light some torches. Wake up all my relatives."

He then asked Roderigo, "Do you think that they are married?"

"Truly, I think they are."

"Oh, Heaven! How did she get out of my house? Her blood is treasonous! Fathers, from now on do not trust that your daughters will continue to be obedient because they have always acted that way — they can change."

He paused and then added, "Aren't there magical charms and love spells that can change the nature of youth and maidenhood? Have you read, Roderigo, of things like that?"

"Yes, sir, I have indeed."

Brabantio said to his servants, "Wake up my brother."

He said to Roderigo, "Now I wish that you had married my daughter."

He said to his servants, "Some of you go one way, some another."

He said to Roderigo, "Where can we apprehend my daughter and the Moor?"

"I think that I can lead you to him, if you want. Get some armed men and come along with me."

"Lead on. At every house I will call and wake up the sleepers. As a person of power and influence, I can demand and get help from almost every house."

He ordered his servants, "Get weapons, and get some special officers of night — not the usual night watchmen — to go with us."

He added, "Good Roderigo, I will reward your actions to me."

On another street of Venice were standing Othello, Iago, and some servants holding torches. Iago was telling Othello a partial truth. He told him the truth about Brabantio's anger toward him, but he lied about his conversation with Roderigo.

Iago said about his conversation with Roderigo, "Although in the trade of war I have slain men, yet I believe it to be immoral to commit cold-blooded murder. I lack sometimes the evil-mindedness to do what would help me. Nine or ten times I was tempted to stab him here under the ribs."

"It is better that you did not," Othello replied.

"But he chattered foolishly and called you such scurvy and provoking terms that, with the little godliness I have, I spared his life with great difficulty."

Iago then began to speak about Brabantio: "But let me ask you, sir, are you securely married? Be assured that this magnifico is much beloved and that he has much power; indeed, his power approaches that of the Duke of Venice. If he can, he will make you get a divorce, or put upon you whatever restraint and hardship the law, with all his might to enforce it, will give him scope."

"Let him act on his spite," Othello said calmly. "The services that I have done for the Venetian government will outweigh his complaints — my services will speak louder than his complaints. People do not know, because I won't boast until boasting is honorable, that I am descended from men of royal rank, and my family, in all due modesty, is equal in social status to the family that I have married into. Know, Iago, that I love the gentle Desdemona. If I did not, I would not have married her and given up my freedom in the tents of military camps for the restrictions and confinements of marriage — even if marrying her would have given me all the treasures of sunken ships lying on the bottom of the sea. But look! What lights are coming toward us?"

"Those are the lights of Desdemona's awoken father and his friends," Iago replied. "It is best — and safer — for you to go inside."

"No," Othello said. "I must confront them. My good qualities, legal right, and blameless soul shall serve me well. Are you sure that these people are Desdemona's father and his friends?"

Looking again, Iago said, "By Janus, I think they are not."

Iago thought, *Janus is a literally two-faced Roman god. Since I am figuratively two-faced, Janus is an appropriate god for me to swear by.*

Michael Cassio and some other military officers carrying torches arrived.

Othello greeted them, "The servants of the Duke, and my lieutenant, welcome. May the goodness of the night be upon you, friends! What is the news?"

"The Duke greets you, general," Cassio said. "And he urgently requires your immediate appearance."

"What is the matter?"

"I think that it is a matter of some urgency that concerns the island of Cyprus. Our ships have sent a dozen messengers, one after the other, this night. Many of the consuls have already been awoken and are meeting at the Duke's. You have been urgently sent for. When you were not found at your lodging, the Venetian Senate sent three different groups of people to find you."

"It is well that you have found me. I will leave a brief message at this inn and then go with you."

Othello went inside the inn.

Cassio asked Iago, "Ancient, what is he doing here?"

"Tonight, he has boarded a treasure-ship on land," Iago replied. "If he can keep the ship, he is a made man forever."

Iago thought, *Yes, Desdemona comes from a wealthy family, and Othello has boarded her — or will board her — in a sexual sense.*

"I do not understand."

"He's married."

"To whom?"

Iago started to answer, "To —" But Othello came out of the building and Iago asked him, "Come, captain, are you ready to go?"

"I'm ready."

Cassio saw some people coming toward them and said, "Here comes another troop of people seeking you."

"It is Brabantio," Iago said. "General, be advised; he comes with bad intent toward you."

Brabantio, Roderigo, and several officers carrying torches came toward Othello.

"Stop!" Othello shouted. "Stand there!"

They stopped, and Roderigo said to Brabantio, "Signior, it is the Moor."

"Arrest him!" Brabantio shouted. "He's a thief!"

Several people, including Iago, drew their swords.

Iago immediately singled out the one person he knew would not hurt him and said, "You, Roderigo! Come, sir, I will fight you."

Iago thought, *Roderigo and I can pretend to fight. That way, I will look as if I am defending the Moor.*

Othello said, "Put away your bright swords, or the dew will rust them."

He thought, *If my sword were to rust, it would be because of blood. The swords that Brabantio and his followers are carrying are in the hands of amateurs.*

He added, "Good signior, you shall command more respect because of your many years than because of your weapons."

"Oh, you foul thief, where have you hidden my daughter?" Brabantio said. "Damned as you are, you have enchanted and bewitched her. My common sense tells me that chains of magic must bind my daughter. Otherwise, a maiden so tender, beautiful, and happy, who is so opposed to marriage that she has shunned the wealthy and darling men of our nation with their curled hair, would never have — thereby incurring public ridicule — run away from her father and her home to the sooty bosom of such a thing as you, who inspires fear, not delight. Let the world judge whether it is obvious that you have used foul charms on her and abused her delicate youth with drugs or poisonous potions that weaken willpower. The court of law will agree that this is probable and easy to believe. I therefore seize and arrest you because you are a corrupter of the world, a magician who practices prohibited and illegal dark arts."

He ordered his followers, "Lay hold of him. If he resists, overpower him at his peril."

"Don't move and don't fight, whether you are on my side or against me," Othello said. "If it were my cue to fight, I would have known it without a prompter."

He then asked Brabantio, "Where do you want me to go so I can answer this charge of yours?"

"I want you to go to prison," Brabantio said, "until a court of law will hear my case."

"Suppose I do that," Othello said, "Will the Duke be happy with that? His messengers are here by my side. They have orders to bring me to him because of some important and urgent business of the state."

One of the Duke's officers said to Brabantio, "That is true, most worthy signior. The Duke is holding a council and you, yourself, I am sure, have been sent for."

"What! The Duke is holding a council! At this time of the night! Bring him away and take him to the Duke. Mine is not an idle cause. The Duke himself and all of my fellow senators cannot but feel this wrong as if it were their own, for if such actions as the Moor's may be done freely, bond-slaves and pagans shall our statesmen be."

They left to see the Duke.

The Duke of Venice and the Venetian senators were sitting at a table in the council chamber. Some military officers were also in attendance.

The Duke said, "These reports lack the consistency that would give them credibility."

"Indeed, they are inconsistent with each other," the first senator said. "My letters say that the Turks have a hundred and seven galleys."

The Duke said, "My letters say a hundred and forty."

The second senator said, "And mine, two hundred. However, although they do not agree on the number of ships — in such cases as this, where estimates are given, disagreement in numbers is common — yet all these letters confirm that a Turkish fleet is sailing to Cyprus."

"That is certainly probable," the Duke said. "The discrepancy in the number of ships does not make me so overconfident that the reports are wrong that I disbelieve the reports' main point: A Turkish fleet is headed toward Cyprus to attack it and take it away from us. That is something that we must be concerned about."

A sailor outside the council chamber called, "I have news!"

The first officer said, "Here is a messenger from the galleys."

The sailor entered the council chamber and said, "The Turkish fleet is now sailing to the island of Rhodes. Signior Angelo ordered me to carry this news to this council."

The Duke asked his advisors, "What do you think about this change in the Turkish fleet's course?"

The first senator said, "That cannot be the truth: Reason shows that the Turks cannot be intending to attack Rhodes. This is a trick; its purpose is to make us concerned about the island of Rhodes and not the island of Cyprus, which must be the Turks' real intended destination. When we consider how much more important Cyprus is to the Turks than Rhodes is, and when we consider that Cyprus is not as well militarily prepared to resist invasion as Rhodes is, then we must realize that the Turks intend to attack Cyprus and not Rhodes. The Turks are not incompetent; they will not leave what is most important until last, and they will not attack a strongly defended island of lesser value to them when they can instead attack a weaker defended island of much greater value to them."

"This is good reasoning based on the best evidence we have," the Duke said. "We can be certain that the Turks do not intend to attack Rhodes."

The first officer, seeing a messenger arriving, said, "Here comes more news."

The messenger arrived and said, "The Turks from the Ottoman Empire, reverend and gracious senators, who have been sailing toward Rhodes, there joined another fleet that is following them."

"I thought so," the first senator said. "How many ships do you guess are in the new fleet?"

"Thirty," the messenger said. "Now they have steered back to their original course and are openly sailing toward Cyprus. Signior Montano, the governor of Cyprus, your trusty and most valiant servant, with honorable respect for you, informs you thus and hopes that you believe him."

"It is certain, now, that the Turks are heading toward Cyprus," the Duke said. "Is Marcus Luccicos in town? He knows much about the Turks and the defense of islands. We should take advantage of the special knowledge that others have."

"He's now in Florence."

"Write from us to him; do this as quickly as possible."

The first senator, seeing more people coming, said, "Here comes Brabantio and the valiant Moor."

Brabantio, Othello, Iago, Roderigo, and some officers arrived.

The Duke of Venice focused his attention on Othello, who was needed now, and said, "Valiant Othello, we must immediately employ you in military matters concerning our general enemy the Ottoman Turks."

Seeing Brabantio, the Duke said, "I did not see you at first; welcome, gentle signior. We lacked your counsel and your help this night."

"And I lacked yours," Brabantio said. "Your good grace, pardon me. Neither my position as senator nor anything I heard of urgent business has raised me from my bed, nor have the ordinary affairs of government aroused me this night. My personal grief overwhelms me like an open flood-gate; its overbearing nature engulfs and swallows all other sorrows — it is not affected by other sorrows."

"Why, what's the matter?" the Duke asked.

"My daughter! Oh, my daughter!"

Some senators asked, "Dead?"

"Yes, to me," Brabantio answered. "She is abused, stolen from me, and corrupted by spells and medicines bought from quack doctors. Human nature, if it is not deficient, blind, or lame of sense, cannot so preposterously err unless witchcraft is involved."

The Duke said, "Whoever he is who in this foul proceeding has thus beguiled your daughter and taken away her senses, and has taken her away from you, the bloody book of law you shall yourself read and interpret in your own way. You will do this even if my own son is the person whom you accuse."

"Humbly I thank your grace," Brabantio said. "Here is the man I accuse: this Moor, whom now, it seems, your special order has brought here on important state business."

A senator said, "We are very sorry to hear it."

The other senators nodded or murmured their agreement with what the senator had said.

The Duke said to Othello, "What, on your own behalf, do you say to this?"

"He can say nothing except to admit that I have spoken the truth," Brabantio said.

"Most mighty, respected, and esteemed signiors," Othello said, "my very noble and approved good masters, that I have taken away this old man's daughter is most true. It is also true that I have married her. The height and breadth of my offense has this extent and no more. Plain am I in my speech, and little blessed with the soft phrase of peace. Ever since these arms of mine had the strength of a seven-year-old until some months ago, they have done their most important work in the tented fields where soldiers fight and sleep, and I can speak of little of this great world unless it pertains to feats of fighting and battle, and therefore little shall I help my cause by speaking for myself. Yet, with your gracious patience, I will tell a plain and unpolished tale describing my whole course of love. I will tell what drugs, what charms, what incantations, and what mighty magic I supposedly used — for such I am accused of using — to win his daughter."

Brabantio said, "My daughter was a maiden who was never bold. She had a spirit so still and quiet that her own natural desires embarrassed her. Could she, in spite of her nature, of their difference in age, of their difference in country of origin, of the danger to her reputation, and of everything, fall in love with something she feared to look at! Only a defective and most imperfect person could think that perfection could so err against all rules of nature; to explain why my daughter eloped with this man, we must look at the practices of cunning Hell. I therefore assert again that he used some drugs that had power over her blood and emotions, or that he gave her a magic love potion that had such an effect on her."

"Suspicion is not proof," the Duke said. "Accusation is not proof without fuller and manifest evidence than the implausible and flimsy evidence and weak probabilities that you are putting forward against him. You need more and better evidence than this if you are to be believed."

The first senator said, "Othello, speak. Did you by cunning and force subdue and poison this young maiden's affection? Or did her affection for you come from her consent and from honest face-to-face conversation with you?"

Othello replied, "Please, send for the lady to come here. She is at the Sagittary Inn. Let her speak about me in the presence of her father. If you find me wicked and guilty after hearing what she says about me, then not only take away the trust I have from you and the office I hold under you, but also sentence me to die."

The Duke ordered, "Bring Desdemona here."

Othello said to Iago, "Ancient, go with them. You best know the location of the inn, and you can lead the Duke's men there."

Iago and two of the Duke's men left.

"Until she comes, I will tell you how she and I fell in love and decided to be married. I will tell you the truth just as if I were confessing my sins to Heaven," Othello said.

The Duke replied, "Speak, Othello."

"Desdemona's father respected me. He often invited me to his home, and he often questioned me about the story of my life: the battles, sieges, and fortunes that I have experienced. I told my story, even from my days of boyhood to the very moment that he bade me tell my story. I spoke about disastrous events, of exciting adventures at sea and on land, of narrow escapes when a gap appeared in the fortifications, of being captured by the insolent foe and sold into slavery, of my ransom out of slavery and my behavior in my travels. I took the opportunity to speak about vast caves and empty, sterile deserts, rough quarries, and rocks and hills whose heads touch Heaven. I also spoke about the cannibals — the Anthropophagi — who eat each other and about hunchbacked men whose heads grow beneath their shoulders. Desdemona intently listened to my story. Sometimes, she would have to leave to attend to household tasks, but she would try to finish these quickly and come to listen to me with a greedy ear. I noticed her interest and took an opportune hour to allow her to ask me to recount my story in full — she had heard bits and pieces of my personal history but not the entire story. I answered her questions, and often as I told her about some distressful event from my youth her eyes filled with tears. When my story was finished, she gave me for my pains a world of sighs. She swore, in faith, that my story was strange, very strange, and it was pitiful, wondrously pitiful. She said that she wished that she had not heard it, but yet she wished that Heaven had made her born not a female but instead such a man as I am. She thanked me, and she requested that if I had a friend who loved her I would teach him how to tell my story, and that story would woo her. Hearing this hint, I spoke my feelings to her. She loved me for the dangers I had experienced, and I loved her because she did pity them. This is the only witchcraft I have used to woo and wed Desdemona. Here comes the lady; let her be my witness that what I have said is true."

Desdemona, Iago, and some attendants arrived.

The Duke said, "I think this tale would win my daughter, too. Good Brabantio, make the best you can out of this mangled matter. Remember this proverb: Men would rather use their broken weapons than their bare hands."

"Please, let my daughter speak," Brabantio said. "If she confesses that she was half the wooer, then may destruction fall upon my head if I wrongly accuse this man."

He said to his daughter, "Come hither, gentle mistress. Do you see in all this noble company the man to whom you most owe obedience?"

"My noble father," Desdemona said, "I do perceive here a divided duty. To you I am bound for my life and education: You raised me. My life and education both have taught me to respect you; you are the lord of duty. I am your daughter, but here is my husband. As much duty as my mother showed to you, giving you preference before her father, so much I claim that I may profess due to the Moor, who is now my lord. To my husband, I most owe obedience, just as my mother did before me."

"May God be with you!" Brabantio said to Desdemona.

He said to the Duke, "I withdraw my accusation against the Moor. Please, your grace, let us move on to the affairs of state."

To himself, he said, "I would prefer to adopt a child than to beget it."

He said to Othello, "Come hither, Moor. I here give you that with all my heart which, if you did not already have it, I would keep from you with all my heart."

He said to his daughter, "Because of you, jewel, I am glad in my soul that I have no other children because your escape would make me a tyrant to them, and I would fasten fetters to their legs to keep them at home."

He said to the Duke, "I have finished speaking, my lord."

The Duke replied, "Let me give you some advice. Perhaps I can say some words that will help these lovers climb into your favor. Our griefs should be over after we see that we have no way to remedy them. We see the worst although we had hoped to avoid it. To continue to mourn a misfortune that is past and gone is the best way to draw new misfortune on. Patient endurance mocks misfortunes that cannot be prevented. The robbed man who smiles steals something from the thief; a man robs himself when he engages in useless grief."

Brabantio replied, "If what you say is correct, then let the Turks cheat us and steal Cyprus from us — the Turks cannot hurt us as long as we smile. A man can hear your words and endure them well when he sits comfortably at home and hears of another's misfortune, but a man who has suffered a misfortune so great that his patience is cruelly taxed must suffer both from the misfortune and from the cruelty of 'comforting' words. These sentences are sugar to a man who does not suffer, but they are gall to a man who does suffer — they are equivocal. But words are merely words; I never yet have heard of any bruised heart that was cured by words heard by the ear. Please, let us now discuss the affairs of the state."

The Duke said, "The Turks with a mighty armed fleet are sailing toward Cyprus. Othello, you best know the fortifications of the place. We have on Cyprus a governor named Montano — he is very competent, yet our general opinion, which determines what we should do, states that you are the better person to hold power on Cyprus in this situation. Therefore, despite your recent marriage, we want you to sail to Cyprus and defend it."

"Because of all my experience in warfare, most grave senators, I regard sleeping on the ground in full armor as equivalent to sleeping on a bed made of the softest down," Othello replied. "I confess that I find a natural and ready eagerness to engage in hardship, and I therefore will undertake to be your general in these present wars against the Turks of the Ottoman Empire.

"Most humbly, therefore, I ask you to make suitable arrangements for my wife. Give her an appropriate residence and financial support with such accommodations and companions as are suitable for someone with her social position."

"If you please," the Duke said, "she shall stay at her father's."

Brabantio said, "I will not have her stay with me."

"Nor will I allow her to stay with her father," Othello said.

"I decline to stay with my father," Desdemona said. "I do not want to upset him, which would happen each time he looked at me. Most gracious Duke, listen with a favorable ear to my proposal and give me permission to do what my lack of sophistication asks from you."

"What do you want, Desdemona?" the Duke asked.

"I love the Moor and want to live with him," she replied. "My violation of normal standards of conduct and the disruption of my life provide unmistakable proof of that to the world. My heart is now completely in accord with my husband's profession as soldier. I saw Othello's true being in his mind, and I have dedicated my whole being and future to his honor and military virtues. This means, dear lords, that if I am left behind in Venice as a moth — an idler or parasite — of peace whose expenses are paid for by the state, and Othello goes to the war, the rites — both the rites of war and the rights of marriage that follow from the rite of marriage — for which I love him are bereft me. His absence will cause me to be sorrowful until I see him again. Therefore, let me go with him to Cyprus."

Othello said, "Let her have your permission. Vouch with me, Heaven, that I am not begging that she be allowed to go with me only to please the palate of my sexual appetite and to satisfy my lust — I am a mature man, and I do not allow youthful emotions to rule me, although I will of course have the distinct and proper satisfaction of sex within the marriage. I want to be generous and bountiful to — and enjoy — her mind. Heaven forbid that your good souls think that I will ignore your serious and great business while she is with me. No, if winged Cupid's feathered arrows should ever blind me to my duty and make my powers of perception and intelligence dull from excessive sexual activity so that I no longer do the work you expect me to do, then let housewives take my helmet and use it as a cooking vessel and let all unworthy and base adversities form an army and make war against my reputation!"

"You may make the decision whether Desdemona stays here in Venice or goes with you to Cyprus," the Duke said. "But this situation is urgent, and it requires haste. You must leave tonight."

"Tonight, my lord?" Desdemona asked.

"This very night," the Duke replied.

"I will leave tonight with all my heart," Othello said.

The Duke said to the senators, "At nine in the morning we will meet again here. Othello, leave some officer behind so that he can bring our commission to you, along with such other important and relevant things that concern you."

"So please your grace, my ancient, Iago, is a man of honesty and trust. I give him the duty to convey my wife to Cyprus. He can also bring whatever else your good grace shall think is necessary to be sent to me."

"Let it be so. Good night to everyone."

The Duke then said to Brabantio, "Noble signior, if virtue no delightful beauty lacks, your son-in-law is far more fair than black."

The first senator said, "*Adieu*, brave Moor. Treat Desdemona well."

"Watch her carefully, Moor," Brabantio said, "if you have eyes to use. She has deceived her father, and she may deceive you."

As the Duke of Venice and the senators left, Othello called after Brabantio, "I swear upon my life that she will be faithful to me!"

Othello then said, "Honest Iago, I must leave my Desdemona with you. Please, let your wife, Emilia, be her attendant. Bring both of them to Cyprus at the best and most convenient time."

He added, "Come, Desdemona. I have only an hour to spend with you and must devote it to love, worldly matters, and instructions. We must use the time well and do what is necessary."

Othello and Desdemona departed, leaving Roderigo and Iago behind, alone.

Roderigo had been thinking and now he said, "Iago —"

"What have you got to say, noble heart?" Iago asked.

"What do you think I should do?"

"Why, go to bed, and sleep."

"I will immediately drown myself."

Iago joked, "If you do, I will stop being friends with you."

He added, "Why would you drown yourself, you silly gentleman!"

"To live is silliness when to live is torment. When our physician is death, then we have a prescription to die."

"This is villainous!" Iago said. "I have looked upon the world for four times seven years — I am twenty-eight years old — and ever since I acquired the ability to distinguish between a benefit and an injury, I have never found a man who knew how to love himself. Before I would say that I would drown myself because I loved some b*tch, I would exchange my body for the body of a lecherous baboon."

"What should I do?" Roderigo asked. "I confess that it is shameful to be so much in love with Desdemona, but I don't have the power to stop loving her."

"Bullsh*t!" Iago said. "We do have power — we ourselves decide what we are and whether we are this way or that way. Remember that Galatians 6:7 says that '*whatsoever a man soweth, that also shall he reap.*' Our bodies are our gardens, and our free will is our gardener. Whether we plant nettles or sow lettuce, whether we plant minty hyssop or throw away thyme as if it were a weed, whether we fill our garden with one kind of herb or with many kinds, whether we have a garden that is unproductive because we are too lazy to tend it or have a productive garden because we manure it and make it fertile through our hard work is up to us. We have the free will to do these things. We have the power to change. Our lives have a pair of scales. In one scale is reason and in the other scale is sensuality. Unless we had reason to counterbalance sensuality, the natural passions and baseness of our natures would lead us to do outrageous actions. Fortunately, we have reason to cool our raging emotions, our carnal stings, our unrestrained lusts — I consider what you call love to be one of our unrestrained lusts."

"Love is nothing but an unrestrained lust? That cannot be the truth!" Roderigo said.

"It is merely a lust of your body that your will has permitted. Come on, be a man! You want to drown yourself! Instead, drown cats and blind puppies. I have told you that I am your friend and I now tell you that I am determined to help you get what you deserve. We are bound together with cables of everlasting toughness. I could never better help you than now. Remember this proverb: Prepare yourself for success. Therefore, sell your land and put money in your wallet. You can use the money to buy gifts and give them to me to pass on to Desdemona."

Yes, do that, Iago thought. *I will keep the valuable gifts, not give them to Desdemona.*

Iago continued, "Go to Cyprus, the battleground of the current war. Cover your handsome face with a fake beard."

Yes, do that, Iago thought. *You aren't man enough to grow a real beard.*

Iago continued, "I say again, put money in your wallet. It cannot be that Desdemona should long continue to love the Moor — put money in your wallet — and it cannot be that the Moor should long continue to love Desdemona. Their love had a violent and sudden commencement, and you will see a sudden separation — put money in your wallet. These Moors are changeable in their nature — fill your wallet with money — the food that to him now is as luscious as sweet chocolate shall soon be to him like a bitter apple. Desdemona must soon change her love for a young man — the Moor is older than she is. When she has had enough of his body, she will see that she chose wrongly when she chose an older man. She will find that she must change her lover — therefore, put money in your wallet. If you must damn yourself, find a better way of doing it than drowning. Raise all the money you can. If piety and a frail vow of marriage between a wandering barbarian and an over-sophisticated Venetian woman are not too hard for my wits and all the tribe of Hell, you will enjoy her body; therefore, raise money. F**k drowning yourself! It is absolutely the wrong thing to do. If you must die, it is better for you to sleep with her and be hanged than for you not to sleep with her and be drowned."

"Can I count on you to completely support me as I pursue my goal of sleeping with Desdemona?"

"You can count on me — go and raise money. I have told you often, again and again, that I hate the Moor. My reason for hating him is deeply rooted in my heart — you hate him for no less reason than I do. Let us join together and get revenge against him. If you can make a cuckold out of him, you will feel pleasure and I will be entertained. Time is pregnant with many events to which it will give birth."

Iago then gave Roderigo a military command: "About face!"

Roderigo was not a military man and did understand or execute the order.

Iago added, "Go and provide yourself with money. We will talk more about this tomorrow. *Adieu.*"

"Where shall we meet in the morning?"

"At my lodging."

"I will be there early."

"Go now; farewell. But listen to me, Roderigo."

"What?"

"Talk no more about drowning yourself."

"I have changed my mind. Instead, I am going to go and sell all my land."

Roderigo departed, leaving Iago alone.

Iago thought these things:

Just like I am doing now, I have always made my fool a major source of my income. I would be wasting my intelligence and experience if I were to spend time with a fool such as Roderigo and not gain entertainment and profit.

I hate the Moor. It is commonly thought that he has done what is my duty as a husband to do between my sheets — people think that he has slept with Emilia, my wife. I don't know if that is true, but I will assume that it is true. The Moor has a good opinion of me: That will help me to get revenge on him.

Cassio is a handsome man. Let me see now: How can I prepare to commit a double knavery against Othello and Cassio that will result in my taking Cassio's place as Othello's lieutenant? How, how?

Let's see. After a little time has passed, I can lie to Othello and tell him that Cassio is too familiar with Desdemona. Cassio has an agreeable appearance and a charming manner that can arouse suspicion. He seems designed to persuade women to be unfaithful to their husbands. The Moor is of a free and open nature; he thinks that men are honest who only seem to be honest. I can lead him as tenderly by the nose as jackasses are led.

I have it. I have formed a plan. Hell and night must bring my plan's monstrous birth to the world's light.

CHAPTER 2

— 2.1 —

Montano, the governor of Cypress, was standing with two other gentlemen near a quay that was used for loading and unloading ships at a port in Cypress. One gentleman stood on a high structure and so was able to see farther out at sea than Montano, who asked, "What can you see out at sea?"

"Nothing at all," the first gentleman said. "The sea is tempestuous and rough. I cannot see a sail."

"The wind has been tempestuous on land, too," Montano said. "A fuller blast of wind has never shaken our battlements. If the wind has been as tempestuous at sea, what ships' ribs of oak, when mountainous waves of water melt on them, can hold the mortise and keep their joints together and not be wrecked? What do you think will be the outcome of this?"

The second gentleman said, "The outcome must be a scattering of the Turkish fleet. Stand on the foaming shore and you will see that the waves, rebuked by the shore, seem to pelt the clouds. The wind-shaken waves, which have a mane like some monster, seem to throw water on the stars that make up the burning bear — Ursa Minor — and put out the Guardians — Ursa Minor's two brightest stars that serve as guards to the Pole Star, aka North Star. I have never seen a similar upheaval of the enraged sea."

Montano said, "Unless the Turkish fleet reached shelter in a bay, their ships have sunk and their sailors have drowned. It is impossible that the Turkish fleet has ridden out this storm."

A third gentleman arrived and said, "Good news, lads! The war is over before it started. This desperate tempest has so banged up the Turkish fleet that their plan to wage war cannot be completed. Cassio, the Moor's lieutenant who was on a noble ship of Venice, has seen that most of the Turkish ships have been wrecked or damaged."

"Really! Is this true?" Montano asked.

"Cassio's ship has put in at this port," the third gentleman said. "It is a ship that was fitted out in Verona. Michael Cassio, the warlike Moor Othello's lieutenant, has come on shore. The Moor himself is still at sea and has been commissioned to come to Cyprus and govern it."

"I am glad of it," Montano said. "He will be a worthy governor."

"Cassio, although he is comforted by the wreck of the Turkish fleet, looks sad and prays that the Moor is safe; their ships were separated by the foul and violent tempest," the third gentleman said.

"I pray to Heaven that the Moor is safe," Montano said. "I have served under him, and the man commands like a perfect soldier. Let's go and see the noble ship of Venice that's come in and look for brave Othello until our eyes blur together the ocean and the blue sky."

"Let's go," the third gentleman said. "Every minute other Venetian ships are expected to appear."

Cassio appeared and said, "Thanks, you valiant people of this warlike isle, who so respect the Moor! May the Heavens give him defense against the tempestuous elements because I have been separated from him and left him on a dangerous sea."

"Is his ship seaworthy?" Montano asked.

"His ship is stoutly timbered, and his pilot is competent and has been tested by experience," Cassio said. "Therefore, my hope that he is safe is realistic and not excessively optimistic."

They heard people crying, "A sail! A sail! A sail!"

A fourth gentleman arrived, and Cassio asked him, "What is that noise?"

"The town is empty because everyone is on the edge of the cliff looking for ships at sea. They are crying 'A sail!' because they see a ship."

"I hope that it is the ship of the Moor, who will be governor of Cyprus," Cassio said.

Some soldiers of Cyprus fired guns.

The second gentleman said, "They are firing the guns as a courtesy to welcome friends."

"Please, sir," Cassio said, "go and see who has arrived and then come back and tell us who it is."

"I will," the second gentleman said.

He exited.

Montano asked Cassio, "Good lieutenant, is your general married?"

"Yes, and most fortunately. He has married a maiden who surpasses description and wild rumor. She surpasses the extravagances of written descriptions and in the perfect beauty of her being even transcends the imagination. No matter how well you think of her, she is better than you think."

The second gentleman returned, and Cassio asked him, "Which ship has arrived?"

"The ship carrying Iago, who serves as ancient to the general."

"His ship has had very favorable and happy speed," Cassio said. "The tempests themselves, high seas, and howling winds, the jagged rocks and sandbanks — underwater traitors that hope to damage the guiltless keel — have a sense of beauty and thereby restrain their dangerous nature so that the divine Desdemona may safely sail to her destination."

"Who is this Desdemona?" Montano asked.

"She is the woman I spoke of, our great captain's captain, the wife of Othello, left in the care of the bold Iago, whose arrival here is a week earlier than expected," Cassio said, adding, "Great Jove, guard Othello and swell his sail with your own powerful breath so that he may bless this bay with his tall ship, make love's quick pants in Desdemona's arms, give renewed fire to our depressed spirits, and bring comfort to all Cyprus!"

Desdemona, Emilia, Iago, a newly bearded Roderigo, and some attendants arrived.

Cassio said, "Behold, the ship's wealth — this woman — has come on shore! You men of Cyprus, bend your knees to this woman, whose name is Desdemona. Hail to you, lady! May the grace of Heaven, before you, behind you, and on every side, surround you!"

"Thank you, valiant Cassio," Desdemona said. "What news can you tell me of my lord and husband, Othello?"

"He has not yet arrived," Cassio said. "As far as I know, he is well and will be soon here."

"I am afraid for him," Desdemona said. "How were you separated from him?"

"The great storm of the sea and sky drove our ships apart from each other — but look, a sail!"

They heard people crying "A sail!" and guns firing.

The second gentleman said, "The ship has fired a salute to the citadel. This likewise is a friend."

"Go and find out what you can about the ship," Cassio said.

The second gentleman departed.

Cassio said to Iago, "Good ancient, you are welcome."

He said to Emilia, "Welcome, lady."

He then said to Iago, "Do not take this amiss, good Iago. I am merely observing the rules of etiquette. I was raised to be courteous to ladies. I am from Florence, where courtesy and etiquette are forms of art."

He then gave Emilia, Iago's wife, a brief, chaste kiss.

Cassio's family had raised him to be extraordinarily gallant — kissing and handholding between friends of the opposite sex were socially acceptable.

Iago, who was lower in rank than Cassio and resented it, said, "Sir, if she would give you so much of her lips as she often bestows on me of her tongue, you would soon have enough. My wife often criticizes me."

Desdemona said about Emilia, "You have embarrassed her. She says nothing."

"She says nothing now," Iago replied, "but she is very capable of speech — too capable, in fact. She criticizes me even when she allows me to sleep. But it is true that when she is around your ladyship, she somewhat keeps her tongue still, although she still scolds me in her mind."

Emilia said, "You have little cause to say that."

"Come on," Iago said, "you women are models of virtue when you are out of doors, but you are as noisy as bells in your parlors, you are wildcats in your kitchens, you pretend to be saints when you injure other people, you are devils when you are injured, and you are lazy when it comes to doing housework and enthusiastic while having sex in your beds."

"You are slandering women!" Desdemona said.

"No, this is all true, or else I am a Turk — a non-Christian who is not to be believed. When you get out of bed, you play leisurely, and when you go to bed, you work enthusiastically."

"Poets write praise about their loved ones. I do not want *you* to write 'praise' of me," Emilia said.

"I will not praise you," Iago replied.

Desdemona said, "What would you write about me, if you were to praise me?"

"Gentle lady," Iago said, "do not ask me to praise you because I am nothing if not critical."

"Come on," Desdemona said. "Fulfill my request."

She added, "Has someone gone to the harbor to seek news of incoming ships?"

"Yes, madam," Iago replied.

Desdemona thought, *I am not merry, but I will disguise what I am — a wife who is worried about the safety of her husband — by pretending to be in a merry mood.*

She said, "Come on, how would you praise me?"

"I am thinking about my answer," Iago said, "but indeed my ideas come out of my brain the way that sticky birdlime comes out of woolen fabric — with great difficulty. Still, my Muse is laboring — and now she delivers this idea: If a woman is fair and wise and has beauty and intelligence, she intelligently uses her beauty to get what she wants."

"Well praised! What praise can you give a woman if she is black and intelligent?" Desdemona said.

"If she is black, and also has a wit, she will find a white lover who shall her blackness fit."

"This praise is worse," Desdemona said.

"What praise can you give a woman if she is fair and foolish?" Emilia asked.

"She never yet was foolish who was fair; for even her folly helped her to give birth to an heir," Iago said. "A pretty blonde may be foolish, but men find such foolishness in pretty blondes attractive and so pretty blondes marry and have babies."

"These are old and silly jokes to make fools laugh in the alehouse," Desdemona said. "What miserable praise do you have for a woman who is foul and foolish? What have you to say if the woman is ugly and foolish?"

"There is no woman so foul and foolish that she cannot use the same tricks that pretty and intelligent women use," Iago said.

"This is heavy ignorance," Desdemona said. "You give the best praise to the worst women. What praise would you give a deserving woman, one who, because she is so good, compels even malicious people to approve of her?"

"She who was always pretty and never proud, spoke well and yet was never loud, never lacked gold and yet never spent excessively on expensive clothing, did not indulge herself even when she could, when angry and able to get revenge nevertheless accepted her injury and rejected her hurt feelings, she who was wise enough never to ignore morality and take advantage of someone by giving them a nearly worthless item such as a cod's head in exchange for a valuable item such as a salmon's tail, she who was wise enough and strong enough never to exchange a penis for a pudendum and become a lesbian, she who could think and yet keep her thoughts secret, she who knew that suitors were following her and yet did not look behind her, she was a person, if ever such person were, to —"

Iago paused, and Desdemona asked, "To do what?"

"— suckle fools and chronicle small beer."

"That is a very lame and impotent conclusion!" Desdemona said. "Is that all that such an excellent woman could and should do! To raise babies and keep household accounts! Babes get either intelligence or foolishness from their mothers' milk. Would such an excellent woman make her babies foolish?"

She said to Emilia, "Do not let Iago be your teacher, although he is your husband."

She added, "What do you think, Cassio? Isn't Iago a most coarse and licentious teacher?"

"He speaks plainly, madam," Cassio said. "You may relish him more as a soldier than as a scholar."

As Cassio spoke, he held Desdemona's hand, something that was acceptable in the society in which he was raised, just like giving a friendly kiss to a married woman he knew.

Iago watched Cassio and thought, *He is taking Desdemona by the hand. Good, Cassio. Now he is whispering to her. With as little a web as this, I will ensnare as great a fly as Cassio. Go on. Smile at her. I will use your own courtly behavior to fetter you.*

He said out loud to Cassio, "You are saying the truth. It is exactly as you say."

He thought, *If such courtly behavior as you are engaging in will strip your lieutenancy away from you, you will regret doing such things as holding and kissing Desdemona's hand, just as you are now doing. You are way too eager to act like a courtly gentleman. Very good, Cassio. You kiss so well! You show Desdemona an excellent courtesy, indeed! Yet again you kiss Desdemona's fingers — I wish that her fingers were the nozzles of enema bags!*

A trumpet sounded, and Iago said out loud, "It is the Moor! I know the distinctive call his trumpeter makes."

Cassio said, "You are right. It is Othello."

"Let's go and greet him," Desdemona said.

"Look, here he comes," Cassio said.

Othello and some attendants arrived.

Othello said to Desdemona, "My beautiful warrior!"

"My dear Othello!" she replied.

"I am extremely happy to see you here — as happy as I am surprised that you arrived on Cyprus before I did. You are the joy of my soul! If after every tempest would come such calms, I wish that the winds would blow until they have awakened death! Let the laboring ship climb hills of seas that are as high as Mount Olympus and then duck again as low as Hell is from Heaven! If it were my time now to die, I would die a very happy man because, I fear, my soul is so filled with such absolute happiness that I shall never again be this happy."

Desdemona replied, "May the Heavens grant that our loves and happiness should increase with each day we live!"

"Amen to that, sweet Heavenly powers!" Othello said. "I cannot speak well enough to describe my happiness — my heart is too filled with joy."

He kissed Desdemona twice and said, "I hope that these kisses are as close to fighting as we will ever come."

Iago thought, *Desdemona and you are like a well-tuned musical instrument now, but I will loosen the pegs of the strings and turn your harmony into discord. You think that I am an honest man, and I honestly intend to ruin your marriage.*

Othello said, "Come, let us go to the castle. We have received good news, friends. The war is over; the Turks have been drowned."

He said to Montano and the other gentlemen of Cyprus, "How are my old friends here on this isle?"

He said to Desdemona, "Honey, you shall be well liked here in Cyprus; I have found great friendship among the people here. Oh, my sweetheart, I am talking too much because I am so happy."

He added, "Please, good Iago, go to the bay and take care of my belongings. Bring the captain of the ship to the citadel. He is a good man, and his worthiness commands much respect."

He added, "Come, Desdemona, once more, we are well met here at Cyprus."

Othello, Desdemona, and most of the others departed.

Iago said to one of the attendants who were leaving, "Meet me soon at the harbor."

Now Iago and Roderigo were alone, and Iago said, "Come here, Roderigo. If you are bold and brave — people say that ordinary men who fall in love acquire a nobility of character that they were not born with — listen to me. Lieutenant Cassio has guard duty tonight — but first let me tell you something important — Desdemona is clearly in love with him."

"Desdemona is in love with Cassio!" Roderigo exclaimed. "That is not possible!"

Iago put his finger to his lips in a "Shush" gesture and said to Roderigo, "Place your finger like this and be quiet so that I can wise you up."

He lowered his finger and said, "You remember how violently Desdemona first loved the Moor, although what she loved him for was his bragging to her and telling her fantastic lies. Will Desdemona continue to love him because he talks foolishly? Don't even think that. Her eye must be fed; she must have someone handsome to look at and to love. The devil is black, and what delight shall Desdemona have when she looks at the Moor and sees the devil? After one has a lot of sex and becomes satiated, there must be, to reignite one's sexual appetite, loveliness in appearance and similarity in age, manners, and virtues. The Moor is deficient in all of these. He is black, he is older than Desdemona, and because he is from another country and culture, he and she are different in other ways as well. Now, because she and the Moor are so dissimilar, Desdemona's delicate tenderness will find itself abused, and she will begin to heave the gorge — that is, vomit. She will disrelish and abhor the Moor; her very nature will reject the Moor and compel her to love some second choice instead of the Moor. Now, sir, this granted — and it must be granted because it is very obvious and natural — who is more likely to be next in line for Desdemona's love than Cassio? He is a knave who is very smooth-tongued. He is conscientious in seeming to be polite and courteous, but only so that he can achieve the fulfillment of his lecherous passions. No one is more likely than he to be the next object of Desdemona's affections. He is a slippery and subtle knave, a finder of opportunities, and a man who has an eye to create opportunities for himself, although true opportunities never present themselves naturally to him — he is a devilish knave. In addition, the knave is handsome, he is young, and he has all those attributes that foolish and immature minds look for. He is a pestilent and complete knave, and the woman has already found him."

"I cannot believe that Desdemona is like that," Roderigo said. "She is blessed and moral."

"Bulls*t!" Iago said. "The wine she drinks is made of grapes. All wines have sediment; all women have faults. If Desdemona were blessed and moral, she would never have loved the Moor. Blessed! You may as well call entrails — where food is no longer food — blessed! Didn't you see her holding hands with him? Didn't you see that?"

"Yes, I did see that, but that was but nothing but courtesy and good etiquette," Roderigo said. "He is from Florence, and Florentines do such things."

"It was lechery — I swear it!" Iago said. "It was a preface and obscure prologue to an upcoming history of lust and foul thoughts. Their lips were so close that their breaths embraced. Villainous thoughts, Roderigo! When these intimacies so lead the way, soon comes the main exercise — the two bodies joined, making the beast with two backs. It's obvious. But, sir, do what I tell you to do. I have brought you from Venice. Stay awake tonight and do what I tell you to do. Cassio, who has guard duty, does not know you. I will be close to you. Find an opportunity to anger Cassio, either by speaking too loud, or disparaging his job performance, or by doing something else that will anger him at the right time."

"Huh," Roderigo said.

"Sir, Cassio is rash and very easy to anger, and he is likely to try to hit you. Provoke him, so that he will attempt violence against you. When that happens, I will cause these citizens of Cyprus to riot; they will not be appeased until Cassio is fired and someone — me — replaces him. That way, you will have a shorter journey to your desires — you will bed Desdemona more quickly — by the means I shall then have to promote your desires. Both you and I will benefit from the firing of Cassio; unless we get rid of him, we cannot be successful in achieving our goals."

"I will do this, if I have the opportunity," Roderigo said.

"You will have the opportunity — I promise," Iago said. "Meet me soon at the citadel. I now must bring the Moor's baggage ashore. Farewell."

Roderigo replied, "*Adieu*," and then he departed.

Alone, Iago thought these things:

That Cassio loves Desdemona, I well believe. That she loves him is plausible and very believable. Women are untrustworthy. I believe that the Moor, although I cannot stand him, is of a faithful, loving, noble nature, but I think that he will cost Desdemona dearly. Truly, I love her, too. I do not love her solely because of lust, although it is certainly possible that I am guilty of the sin of lusting for her. However, I want to sleep with her in part out of revenge. I suspect that the Moor has leapt into my seat — into that part of my wife's body that only I ought to fill. This suspicion gnaws at my insides like a poisonous mineral. Nothing can or shall content my soul until I get even with him. I remember Exodus 21:1 and 21:23-4: '... these are the laws ... life for life, / eye for eye, tooth for tooth.' To that I would add, 'wife for wife.' But if I cannot cuckold the Moor, I can make him so jealous of Desdemona and so certain that she has been unfaithful to him that his intelligence and his reason will not be able to convince him that she is faithful.

Roderigo is poor trash — a worthless person — from Venice. I manage — and restrain as needed, since I am not actually promoting his cause, although he thinks I am — his hunting of Desdemona, and if he does as I tell him to do, soon I will have Michael Cassio at my mercy, which is nonexistent. I will slander Cassio to the Moor and say that Cassio has a lascivious manner. Actually, Cassio does seem to have a lascivious manner — I can easily imagine him wearing my nightcap while he is in bed with my wife. I will make the Moor thank me, respect me, and reward me. For what? For making him egregiously an ass and plotting against his peace and quiet even so far as to make him insane.

My opportunity now is present, but the details are still confused. Knavery's plain face is never seen until it is used.

— 2.2 —

On a street of Cypress, a herald read a proclamation out loud:

"It is the pleasure of Othello, our noble and valiant general, since certain and reliable news has now arrived that the Turkish fleet has been entirely destroyed, that every person enjoy public festivity and revelry. Dance. Make bonfires. Enjoy whatever entertainment your inclination leads you to. In addition to celebrating the destruction of the Turkish fleet, celebrate also the marriage of Othello and Desdemona."

The herald added, "This is the proclamation that Othello wanted to be read out loud. All kitchens and pantries are open, and everyone is invited to feast from now until the bells have tolled eleven. Heaven bless the isle of Cyprus and our noble general, Othello!"

In a hall in the castle, Othello said to Michael Cassio, "Good Michael, be in charge of and keep an eye on the guards tonight. Let us exercise self-control and not revel so much that we are indiscrete."

"Iago has his instructions for what to do, but nevertheless, I will keep my eye on things."

"Iago is a very honest and very good man," Othello said. "Michael, good night. Tomorrow at your earliest convenience meet with me."

To Desdemona, Othello said, "Come, my dear love. We have made our purchase — we have gotten married. However, the fruits are to ensue. Our profit is yet to come between me and you — we have not yet consummated our marriage."

He said to Cassio, "Good night."

Othello, Desdemona, and their attendants departed, and Iago arrived.

Cassio said, "Welcome, Iago; we must go and stand watch."

"Not yet, lieutenant," Iago said. "It is not yet ten o'clock. Our general left us so early because of his love for Desdemona. We cannot blame him for that. He has not yet slept with her, and she would be good sport for Jove, the Roman god who enjoyed many affairs with immortal goddesses and with mortal women."

"She's a most exquisite lady," Cassio replied.

"And I bet that she is vigorous in bed."

"To be sure, she is a most fresh and delicate creature."

"Her eyes are beautiful! I think that they give provocative invitations."

"Her eyes are beautiful, but I think that they are modest, not lascivious."

"When she speaks, doesn't she cause men to feel passion?" Iago asked.

"She is indeed perfection," Cassio said.

"Well, happiness to their sheets!" Iago said.

He thought, *I have tried to tempt Cassio to try to seduce Desdemona, but he is having none of it, although he clearly admires her. Pity.*

Iago said, "Come, lieutenant, I have a jug of wine. Just outside are a couple of Cyprus gallants who would like to drink a toast to the health of black Othello."

"Not tonight, good Iago. I do not have a good head for alcohol — I am easily intoxicated. I wish that society had a different and better — and yet polite — way of celebrating than drinking."

"The men outside are our friends," Iago said. "Have one cup of wine with them. I will do most of the drinking for you."

"I have drunk only one cup of wine tonight, and that was secretly and carefully diluted with water, too, but I — and probably you — can tell that it has affected me. I am unfortunate in that I cannot tolerate alcohol, and I dare not drink any more wine."

"What, man! This is a night of revels and parties — we are celebrating! The gallants I mentioned want you to celebrate with them."

"Where are they?"

"Just outside the door; please, call them in."

"I will do it, but I dislike it," Cassio said.

He left to invite the people outside to come in.

Iago thought, *If I can persuade Cassio to drink one more cup of wine in addition to the cup that he has already drunk tonight, he will be as ready to fight and to take offense as a young lady's feisty pet dog. Already, that lovesick fool Roderigo, whom love has almost turned inside out, has drunk many toasts in honor of Desdemona. He is awake and watching for his opportunity to get Cassio in trouble. Three lads of Cyprus, noble swelling spirits, who are touchy about the respect that they think is due them and who are characteristic of the men on this warlike isle, are already drunk with the full and flowing cups of wine I have given them. They will be guards tonight, too, along with Montano, the former governor of Cyprus. I will put Cassio in the midst of this flock of drunkards and make him commit an action that will outrage the citizens of this isle. Here Cassio and the three young drunks come. Soon Roderigo will arrive. If my plot has the consequences it should, my boat will sail freely with a favorable wind and current — I will enjoy success.*

Cassio returned. With him were the three young men whom Iago had already gotten drunk and Montano, the former governor of Cyprus. The three young men and Montano would serve as guards this night. Servants carrying wine also entered the room.

Cassio said, "By God, they have already given me some wine, which I have drunk."

Montano said, "Just a little wine, I swear — not more than a pint, as I am a soldier."

Iago called to a waiter, "Bring some wine!"

He then began to sing a song to which he and others clinked their tankards together:

"*And let me the tankard clink, clink;*

"*And let me the tankard clink.*

"*A soldier's a man;*

"*A life's but a span;*

"*Why, then, let a soldier drink.*"

He then said, "Some wine, boys!"

Cassio, made drunk by only two servings of wine, one of them diluted with water, said, "That is an excellent song."

"I learned it in England," Iago said, "where, indeed, they are most expert in drinking. Your Dane, your German, and your sagging-bellied Hollander — waiter, bring more wine! — are nothing compared to your English."

"Is an Englishman so expert in his drinking?" Cassio asked.

"Why, he drinks, easily, until and after your Dane is dead drunk; he does not have to sweat to outdrink your German; your Hollander will vomit while the Englishman's tankard is being refilled."

Cassio cried, "To the health of our general!"

"Good toast," Montano said. "I will drink to that."

Iago sang again:

"*Oh, sweet England!*

"*King Stephen was a worthy peer,*

"*His breeches cost him a crown;*

"*He held them sixpence all too dear,*

"*With that he called the tailor low-down.*

"*He was a man of high renown,*

"*And you are of low degree.*

"*It is extravagant clothing that pulls the country down,*

"*So wrap your old cloak around you.*"

Cassio said, "Why, this is a more exquisite song than the other one."

"Will you hear it again?" Iago asked.

"No — because I hold a man to be unworthy of his position who does such things as drinking, singing, and carousing. Well, God's above all; and some souls must be saved, and some souls must not be saved."

"That's true, good lieutenant," Iago said.

"For my own part — no offence to the general, or to any man of rank — I hope to be saved," Cassio said.

"And so do I, lieutenant."

"Yes, but, by your leave, I hope that you are not saved before me," Cassio said. "According to military protocol, the lieutenant must be saved before the ancient because he outranks him. But let's have no more of this; let's attend to our affairs. We have a job to do: guard duty. May God forgive us our sins! Gentlemen, let's attend to our business. We have guard duty. Do not think, gentlemen, that I am drunk. I know what I ought to know. This is my ancient; this is my right hand, and this is my left hand. I am not drunk now; I can stand well enough, and I can speak well enough."

An impartial observer might think, *Cassio, you are unsteady on your feet and you are slurring your words*, but the men with Cassio said, "You are excellent and well."

"Why, so I am," a drunken Cassio said. "I am also not drunk."

He departed.

"Let us go to the ramparts, men, and start our guard duty," Montano said.

The three young men of Cyprus followed after Cassius.

Montano would have gone, too, but Iago spoke to him, saying, "That drunken fellow who left before the three young men is a soldier fit to be Caesar's right-hand man and give military commands, but he has a vice that is the equal of his virtue. They form a perfect equinox; his vice is as black as his virtue is fair. It is a pity. I fear the trust that Othello has in him. Sometime in the future, this fellow is likely to do something that will hurt this island."

"Is he often drunk?" Montano asked.

"He gets drunk every night before he sleeps. If his drunkenness did not put him to sleep, he would stay awake a couple of days in a row."

"This is something that the Moor, our general, should be made aware of," Montano said. "Perhaps he does not know about it, or perhaps he so prizes the virtues that are in Cassio that he ignores his vice. That seems likely."

Roderigo entered the room, and Iago whispered to him so that Montano could not hear, "You have come at a good time. Cassio just left; go after him. You know what to do."

Montano continued, "It is a great pity — and a great danger — that the noble Moor should have as second in command someone with such a vice as drunkenness. It would be a good deed to tell the Moor that."

"I won't — not even for all of this island!" Iago said. "I respect Cassio, and I would do much to cure him of his vice —"

Noises sounded, and someone shouted, "Help! Help!"

Iago asked, "— but what is going on?"

Roderigo, chased by Cassio, ran into the room.

Cassio, drunk and angry, shouted at him, "You rogue! You rascal!"

Montano asked, "What's the matter, lieutenant?"

"This knave is trying to teach me my duty! He is trying to tell me how to do my job! I'll whip the knave until the marks on his skin resemble a bottle covered with wickerwork."

"Will you whip me?" Roderigo shouted.

"Stop babbling, rogue," Cassio ordered, hitting Roderigo.

Montano said, "Stop, good lieutenant." He grabbed Cassio's hand and added, "Please, sir, stop hitting this man."

"Let me go, sir," Cassio said, "or I'll hit you on the head."

"Come, come, you're drunk," Montano said.

"Drunk!" Cassio said.

He attacked Montano, who fought back.

Iago said quietly to Roderigo so that no one could hear, "Go out, and cry that there is a mutiny, an insurrection."

Roderigo left to carry out Iago's command.

Iago then pretended to be a peacemaker: "Good lieutenant ... for pity, gentlemen ... help! ... lieutenant, sir ... Montano, sir ... help! ... this is an excellent watch — not!"

An alarm bell rang.

Iago shouted, "Who is ringing the bell? ... Diablo — the devil! ... The townspeople will start a riot. ... For God's sake, lieutenant, stop fighting! You will be disgraced forever."

Othello and some attendants entered the room.

"What is the matter here?" Othello asked.

"Damn! I am bleeding! I am likely to die!" Montano said.

"Everyone, stop fighting, if you value your lives," Othello ordered.

Iago said, "Everyone, stop fighting! ... Lieutenant Cassio, sir ... Montano ... gentlemen! Have all of you forgotten all sense of dignity and duty? Stop! The general is speaking to you! Stop! Stop, for the love of God!"

"What is going on here?" Othello said. "What is the cause of this disturbance? Have we all become Turks, and are we going to fight ourselves although Heaven sent a tempest to prevent the real Turks from fighting us? For Christian shame, stop this barbarous brawl! He who angrily moves next to attack someone values his own soul only lightly — he will die as soon as he makes a move! Silence that dreadful bell! It frightens the citizens of this isle and destroys its normal peace and quiet. What is the matter, people? Honest Iago, you who look as if you will die with grief, speak. Tell me who began this fight. Loyal soldier, I order you to tell me."

"I do not know who started the fight," Iago replied. "Everyone seemed to be friends until just now in their conduct. They were like a bride and a groom undressing in preparation for bed, and then, just now, as if some malignant planet of astrology had driven these men out of their minds, they took out their swords and made each other's chests their targets in a bloody fight. I cannot identify any cause of this senseless quarrel, and I would prefer that I had lost my legs in a glorious battle than that they brought me to this quarrel."

"How is it, Michael, that you have this night forgotten the right and honorable way to act?" Othello asked Cassio.

"Please, pardon me," Cassio replied. "I cannot speak in my defense."

"Worthy Montano, you are accustomed to be law-abiding," Othello said. "Everyone has noticed the gravity and sober behavior of your youth, and people of the wisest judgment praise you greatly. What is the reason you are willing to act in such a way as to exchange your good reputation for the bad reputation of a night-brawler? You are spending the wealth of your reputation on trifles. Answer me."

"Worthy Othello, I am seriously injured," Montano said. "Iago, your officer, can inform you about this fight — I should not talk because talking causes me pain — and about my actions. I know of nothing that I have said or done wrong this night unless valuing one's life is sometimes a vice, and defending ourselves is a sin when someone violently attacks us."

"By Heaven, my anger begins to overwhelm my reason. My strong feelings, having shut down my best judgment, now begin to control me," Othello said. "If I move in any way, or lift this arm, even the best and highest ranking of you shall feel my anger. Tell me how this foul rout began and who started it. Whoever is guilty of this offence, even if he were my twin brother, will lose my friendship. What a way to act! Here we are in a town that was a target of the Turkish enemy, the people are still riled up and afraid, and yet you are fighting in a private and domestic quarrel, at night, and while you are on guard duty! This behavior is monstrous! Iago, who began this fight?"

Montano put his hand on Iago's arm and said, "If you deliver more or less than the truth, you are no soldier. Do not let your friendship with Cassio bias you."

"Don't touch me, but you do know me well," Iago said. "I would rather have my tongue cut from my mouth than use it to do offence to Michael Cassio. However, I persuade myself that to speak the truth will not harm him. This is what I know, general. While Montano and I were talking, a fellow came in this room crying out for help. Cassio was chasing him with his sword drawn, determined to use it. Sir, this gentleman, Montano, stepped in and spoke to Cassio, and entreated him to be calm. I myself pursued the fellow who was crying out for help because I was afraid that his cries — as in fact did happen — would frighten the citizens of this town. The fellow was swift of foot and outran me. I returned to this room rather than try to follow him because I heard the clink and fall of swords and Cassio swearing mightily — something I had never heard him do before this night. When I came back — I was away only a short time — I found them fighting together, trading blow and thrust. They were fighting exactly as you saw when you yourself separated them. More of this matter I do not know, but men are men; the best sometimes forget themselves. Though Cassio did some little wrong to Montano, as men in rage strike those who wish them best, yet surely Cassio, I believe, received from the man who fled some strange indignity or insult that a man could not honorably ignore."

"I know, Iago, that your honesty and respect for Cassio affect the way you are telling your story," Othello said. "You are deliberately minimizing Cassio's fault."

He said to Cassio, "I respect your virtues, but you will no longer be an officer of mine."

Desdemona now arrived, accompanied by a few attendants.

Othello said, "Look! My gentle love has been awakened by this commotion."

He said to Cassio, "I will make an example of you."

"What's the matter?" Desdemona said.

"All's well now, sweetheart," Othello said. "Go back to bed."

He said to Montano, "Sir, I myself will pay a doctor to look after your injuries."

Some people helped Montano leave the room and seek the services of a doctor.

Othello said, "Iago, go throughout the town and calm anyone whom this brawl has upset."

He added, "Come, Desdemona. It is normal in the soldiers' life to have their balmy slumbers waked with strife."

Everyone departed except for Iago and Cassio.

Iago asked, "Are you hurt, lieutenant?"

"Yes, and a doctor cannot help me."

"Heaven forbid!"

"Reputation, reputation, reputation!" Cassio cried. "Oh, I have lost my reputation! I have lost the immortal part of myself, and what remains is bestial. My reputation, Iago, I have lost my reputation!"

"As I am an honest man, I thought that you had received some bodily wound; that would hurt you more than a wounded reputation. Reputation is an idle and very false concept. It is often gotten without merit, and it is often lost without just cause. You have lost no reputation at all, unless you regard yourself as such a loser. Remember this proverb: A man is weal — happy — or woe — sorrowful — as he thinks himself so. What, man! There are ways to regain the general's good opinion of you. You are cast aside now only because he is angry, and this punishment is in accordance more with policy than with malice. It is like someone beating his innocent dog in order to frighten an imperious lion. Othello is making an example of you so that his troops and the citizens of Venice will respect his authority. If you plead to him to give you your job back, he will do so."

"I would prefer to be despised than to deceive so good a commander with so slight, so drunken, and so indiscreet an officer as I have been tonight," Cassio said. "Drunk? And speak nonsense like a parrot? And squabble? Swagger? Swear? And talk rubbish to my own shadow? Oh, you invisible spirit of wine, if you have no name that you are known by, let us call you devil!"

"Who was he whom you chased with your sword drawn?" Iago asked. "What had he done to you?"

"I don't know."

"How can that be possible?"

"I remember a mass of things, but nothing distinctly. I remember a quarrel, but not what the quarrel was about. Oh, God, how is it possible that men should put an enemy — wine — in their mouths that will steal away their brains! How is it possible that we should, with joy, pleasure, revel, and the desire for applause, transform ourselves into beasts!"

"Why, you are sober enough now," Iago said. "How is it that you are now thus recovered?"

"It has pleased the devil drunkenness to give place to the devil wrath," Cassio said. "My anger drove out my drunkenness. One imperfection gave way to another, and both make me frankly despise myself."

"Come, you are too hard on yourself," Iago said. "Considering the time, the place, and the condition of this country, I wish that this had not happened to you, but since it has, solve this problem and make things right again for yourself."

"If I ask him to give me my job back, he shall tell me that I am a drunkard!" Cassio said. "Had I as many mouths as Hydra, the nine-headed serpent that Hercules killed, such an answer would stop them all. To be now a sensible and intelligent man, and then a fool, and then a beast! Oh, strange! Every cup of wine too much is cursed and the contents include a devil."

"Come, come, good wine is a good familiar creature, if it be well used — exclaim no more against it," Iago said.

He thought, *That is true, and it is also true that good wine is a bad familiar creature — a witch's personal devil-servant, usually in the form of an animal — if it is badly used.*

Iago added, "Good lieutenant, I think that you know that I am your friend."

"I know it well and have good evidence of it, sir," Cassio said. "I can't believe that I got drunk!"

"You or any other living man may at times be drunk," Iago said. "I'll advise you what you shall do. Our general's wife, Desdemona, is now the general in this respect: The Moor has devoted and given up himself to the contemplation, observation, and noting of her qualities and graces. Confess freely to her what has happened and beg her to help you get your job again. Desdemona is of so generous, so kind, so helpful, and so blessed a disposition that she thinks that it is a sin not to do more than is requested of her. Ask her to mend this break between Othello and you. I will make a bet that she will help you. This break will be mended and your friendship with the Moor will be made stronger than before, just like a bone that has healed after being broken is stronger than it was before it was broken."

"You advise me well," Cassio said.

"I do so because of the sincere friendship I have for you and the honest kindness I feel for you."

"I well believe it," Cassio said. "Early in the morning, I will beg the virtuous Desdemona to plead my case to her husband. My future is desperate if I don't get my job back."

"You are doing the right thing," Iago said. "Good night, lieutenant. I must resume my guard duty."

"Good night, honest Iago," Cassio said.

He departed.

Iago thought, *How can anyone say that I am a villain when this advice I give is open and generous and honest, reasonable, and in fact exactly what is needed for Cassio to get in the good graces of the Moor again? It is very easy to persuade the generous and sympathetic Desdemona to take one's side in a good cause. She is naturally as generous as the Earth that freely gives us oxygen and water. She can easily persuade the Moor to do what she wants him to do. Even if she wanted him to renounce his Christian religion and his baptism and all other seals and symbols of redeemed sin, his soul is so chained to her love that she may create, ruin, and do what she wishes. The Moor's weak willpower will make his sexual appetite for her his god. Can I be considered a villain when I advise Cassio to do what I want him to do — when what I advise is something that will lead to something good for him? This is the divinity of Hell! When devils want to do the blackest sins, the devils mislead people by appearing Heavenly. That is what I am doing now. While this honest fool, Cassio, pleads for help from Desdemona to regain his job, and she pleads for him strongly to the Moor, I will pour poison into the Moor's ear. I will tell him that Desdemona pleads for Cassio because she lusts for him. The more she strives to do Cassio good, the more she shall undo the Moor's love for her. So will I turn her fair virtue into black pitch, and out of her own goodness will I make the net that shall enmesh them all.*

Roderigo now entered the room.

"How are you, Roderigo?" Iago asked.

"I am like a dog that follows in a hunting chase," Roderigo said. "I am not one of the dogs that sniffs out the prey, but merely one of the dogs who barks in the pack — I am an also-ran. I desire Desdemona, but I am not in the running for her affection. My money is almost spent, I have been tonight exceedingly well beaten by Cassio, and I think the conclusion will be that I shall have much experience and nothing else for my pains, and so, with no money at all and a little more sense, I shall return again to Venice."

"How poor are they who lack patience!" Iago said. "What wound did ever heal but by degrees? You know that we work by intelligence and cunning wit, and not by witchcraft — cunning wit depends on dawdling time. To achieve your goal of sleeping with Desdemona will take time. Aren't things going well? Cassio did beat you, but by that small hurt, you have gotten Cassio fired. Many plants grow well in the sunshine, but whatever blossoms first will ripen first. The firing of Cassio is the blossom, and the fruit you desire will follow. You will sleep with Desdemona, but for now be content and peaceful. Look, the sky is lightening; it is morning. Pleasure and action make the hours seem short and time pass quickly. Go to bed; go to your lodging. Go away, I say. We will talk later, but for now go to bed."

Roderigo departed.

Iago thought, *Two things are to be done. One: My wife, Emilia, must plead for Cassio to her mistress, Desdemona. I will tell her to do that. Two: Meanwhile, I must draw the Moor aside and then bring him back when he will see Cassio asking Desdemona for her help. Aye, that's the way. Dull not an evil scheme by coldness and delay. I am willing and eager to put my plot in action.*

CHAPTER 3

— 3.1 —

Cassio and some musicians walked to a place in front of the castle.

Cassio said, "Musicians, play here; I will pay you. Play something that's brief, and bid the Moor, 'Good morning, general.'"

Although Cassio was no longer Othello's lieutenant, he was doing something considerate for Othello and Desdemona: He was following the custom of awakening the newly married couple with music after their first night together.

A clown, aka Fool, aka comedian, arrived, and listened to the musicians.

The clown said, "Your musical instruments have a nasal sound; they sound as if they are making music in a nose. Have your instruments been in Naples?"

The clown thought, *That is a good joke, although I doubt if these musicians will get it. Naples is known for the venereal disease syphilis, which deforms the nose by collapsing the bridge.*

The first musician said, "What do you mean?"

The clown then asked, "Are these wind instruments?"

"Yes, sir, they are," the first musician replied.

"Thereby hangs a tail," the clown said.

"Whereby hangs a tale, sir?" the first musician asked.

"A tail hangs by many a wind instrument that I know," the clown replied.

The clown thought, *That is true. One meaning of wind is a fart, and therefore an anus is a wind instrument. A tail — or penis — hangs by half of the human wind instruments on this Earth.*

The clown added, "Musicians, here's money for you. The general likes your music so well that he desires you, for love's sake, to make no more noise with your instruments."

"Well, sir, we will not," the first musician said.

"If you have any music that cannot be heard, then play it, but the general does not care to actually hear music."

"We have no music that cannot be heard, sir," the first musician said.

"Then put your pipes in your bag and carry them away," the clown said. "You need not carry me away; I will leave on my own. Vanish into air! Go away!"

The musicians departed, and Cassio asked the clown, "Do you hear, my honest friend?"

Because he was from Florence, Cassio's language differed slightly from that of both Venice and Cyprus. He meant, *Will you listen to me, my honest friend?*

The clown ignored the comma in Cassio's question and said, "No, I don't hear your honest friend; I hear you."

"Please, don't engage in word play," Cassio said. "Here is a small gold coin for you. If the gentlewoman — Emilia — who attends the general's wife is stirring, tell her that a man named Cassio entreats her to listen to a few words. Will you do this for me?"

"She is stirring, sir," the clown said.

He thought, *Yes, she is stirring — in more ways than one. She stirs up sexual desire in men, and she is awake and out of bed.*

He also thought, *This is a man who is a little too fancy with words: "entreats her to listen to a few words." Yech!*

Making fun of Cassio's speech, the clown added, "If she will stir hither, I shall seem to notify unto her."

"Do that, my good friend."

The clown departed.

Iago now arrived.

"You have come at a good time, Iago," Cassio said.

"Haven't you been to bed?" Iago asked.

"Why, no," Cassio replied. "The dawn had broken before we parted. I have made bold, Iago, to send a request in to your wife. I want to ask her if she will arrange for me to talk to Desdemona."

"I will send my wife to talk to you very soon," Iago said. "I will also find a way to draw the Moor out of the way so that you and my wife can talk more freely."

"I humbly thank you," Cassio replied.

Iago departed, and Cassio said, "Iago could not be kinder and more honest; he is as kind and honest as a Florentine — a person from my own city, which is known for its etiquette and courtesy."

An impartial observer might remember that Machiavelli, author of *The Prince*, had lived in Florence.

Emilia, Iago's wife, walked up to Cassio.

"Good morning, good lieutenant," she said. "I am sorry that you have incurred the Moor's displeasure, but all will surely be well. The general and his wife were talking about you, and she spoke up for you strongly. However, the Moor replied that the man you hurt is well known in Cyprus and is a member of an important family. Therefore, the wisest thing for the Moor to do was to punish you, but the Moor said that he respects you and he needs nothing more than that respect to reinstate you as his lieutenant when he has a good opportunity to do so."

"Still, I beg you," Cassio replied, "if you think it fitting, and if it may be done, to allow me to speak briefly to Desdemona."

"Please, come in," Emilia replied. "I will put you in a place where you can speak freely to Desdemona."

"I am much obliged to you," Cassio said.

— 3.2 —

In a room of the castle, Othello, Iago, and some gentlemen were speaking about official business.

Othello said, "Iago, give these letters to the pilot of the ship sailing to Venice, and have him give my respects to the senate. Once that is done, come back to me. I will be walking on the fortifications."

Iago replied, "My good lord, I will do what you say."

"Shall we see this fortification, gentlemen?"

"We will go with you, your lordship," a gentleman said.

In the garden of the castle, Desdemona, Cassio, and Emilia were talking. Emilia was serving as Desdemona's chaperone.

Desdemona said, "Be assured, good Cassio, that I will do everything I can to help you regain your position as lieutenant."

"Good madam, do so," Emilia said. "I know that Cassio's misfortune grieves my husband, Iago, as badly as if it had happened to him."

"Iago is an honest man," Desdemona said. "Do not doubt, Cassio, that I will soon have my husband and you together again as friendly to each other as you were before."

"Generous madam," Cassio said, "whatever shall become of Michael Cassio, he will never be anything but your true servant."

"I know it," Desdemona said. "I thank you. You do respect my husband. You have known him a long time. Be well assured that he shall be estranged from you no longer than is politically expedient. He needed to make an example of you."

"Yes," Cassio said, "but, lady, that political expediency may either continue so long, or continue because of weak and trivial reasons, or continue because of accidental, unrelated political events, that with myself absent and with someone else filling in as lieutenant, the general will forget his and my friendship and my service to him."

"Don't think that," Desdemona said. "With Emilia as a witness, I promise you that you will regain your position as lieutenant. I assure you that if I promise to do something for a friend that I will do everything that I have promised." She joked, "My husband will never rest: I'll keep him awake just like I were taming a hawk. I will talk to him and nag him until he grows impatient. His bed shall seem like a school because of the lectures that I will give him, and when he eats his meals he will think that it is as if he were a priest hearing a long confession. Whatever he does, I will bring up Cassio's petition to be reinstated as lieutenant. Therefore, be happy, Cassio. I will be the lawyer who pleads your case to Othello, and I would rather die than give up your cause."

Emilia saw Othello and her husband, Iago, entering the garden, and said, "Madam, here comes my lord."

Cassio said to Desdemona, "Madam, I'll leave now."

"Why, stay, and hear me speak to my husband about you," she replied.

"Madam, not now," Cassio said. "I am very ill at ease, and I am not prepared to plead to be reinstated."

"Well, do what you think best," Desdemona said.

Cassio departed.

Iago saw Cassio and said, quietly but deliberately loud enough for Othello to hear, "I don't like that."

"What did you say?" Othello asked.

"Nothing, my lord, but — I don't know what I was saying."

"Wasn't that Cassio who just left my wife?" Othello asked.

"Cassio, my lord!" Iago said. "No, surely. I cannot think that it was he. Why would he steal away so guilty-like when he saw that you were coming?"

"I do believe that it was Cassio," Othello said.

"How are you, my lord?" Desdemona greeted Othello. "I have been talking with a man here, a man who languishes because you are displeased with him."

"Who is it you mean?"

"Why, your lieutenant, Cassio," Desdemona replied. "My good lord, if I have any grace or power to move you, please be reconciled with him immediately. For if he is not someone who truly respects you, someone who has erred in ignorance and not on purpose, then I cannot judge who is honest. Please, call him back and be reconciled with him."

"Was that Cassio who left just now?" Othello asked.

"Yes," Desdemona replied. "He was so mournful that he left part of his grief with me, and I suffer with him. Good love, be reconciled with him."

"Not now, sweet Desdemona. Some other time."

"But shall it be shortly?"

"The sooner, sweetheart, for you."

"Shall it be tonight at supper?"

"No, not tonight."

"Tomorrow during the noon meal, then?"

"I shall not dine at home; I am meeting the captains at the citadel."

"Why, then, tomorrow night, or Tuesday morning, or Tuesday noon, or Tuesday night, or Wednesday morning. Please, name the time that you will be reconciled with Cassio, but let it not exceed three days. Truly, he's penitent, and yet his trespass, ordinarily, is almost not severe enough to incur a private rebuke, much less a public disgrace. Of course, it is understandable that in times of military struggle, you must make an example, when necessary, of even high-ranking officers.

"But when shall Cassio come and be reconciled to you? Tell me, Othello. I wonder in my soul what you could possibly ask me to do that I would refuse to do, or would put off with stammering.

"Remember what a friend Michael Cassio has been to you. He used to come with you when you wooed me, and whenever I disparaged you, he stood up for you and praised you."

Desdemona thought, *I used to disparage you on purpose just to hear Cassio defend you and praise you.*

She added, "Is it really such a difficult decision to forgive his fault and bring him into your favor again?"

"Please, say no more," Othello said. "I will be reconciled to Cassio, and soon. He can come and see me whenever he wishes. I will deny you nothing."

"Why, I am not asking for something that will benefit myself," Desdemona said. "What I am asking for now is similar to asking you to put on your gloves when needed, or eat nourishing food, or wear warm clothing on cold days, or to do something else that benefits yourself. Being reconciled with Cassio means that you will have a good and competent lieutenant again. When I have a request that will put your love for me to the test, that request will be serious and heavy and fearful to be granted."

"I will deny you nothing," Othello said. "But now, please, grant me this request: Leave me and let me be by myself for a while."

"Shall I deny you your request?" Desdemona said. "No, of course not. Farewell, my lord."

"Farewell, my Desdemona. I'll come to you soon."

Desdemona said, "Emilia, let's go."

She said to Othello, her husband, "Do whatever you want to do. Whatever you do, I am and will be your obedient wife."

Desdemona and Emilia departed.

Othello said to himself, with affection for his wife, "Excellent wench! Damn, but I do love you. If I should ever stop loving you, chaos, from which the world arose and to which it will return at the end of time, will come again."

"My noble lord," Iago said.

"What is it, Iago?"

"Did Michael Cassio, when you were wooing Desdemona, know about your love for her?"

"He did, from the beginning to the ending of my wooing her. Why do you ask?"

"To satisfy my curiosity," Iago said. "No other reason."

"Why are you curious about that, Iago?"

"I did not think he had been acquainted with her."

"He was, and he very often served as a messenger between us."

"Indeed!" Iago said.

"Indeed!" Othello repeated. "Yes, indeed. Do you see anything odd about that? Isn't Cassio an honest man?"

"Honest, my lord!"

"Honest!" Othello repeated. "Yes, honest."

"My lord, for all I know, he is honest."

"What are you thinking?" Othello asked.

"Thinking, my lord?"

"Thinking, my lord?" Othello repeated. "By Heaven, you keep echoing me as if there were some monstrous thought in your brain that is too hideous to be revealed. You are thinking something. I heard you say just now that you didn't like it when you saw Cassio leaving my wife. What didn't you like? And when I told you that Cassio knew all my thoughts when I was wooing Desdemona, you said, 'Indeed!' And you furrowed your brow as if you had some horrible idea shut up in your brain. If you are my friend, tell me what you are thinking."

"My lord, you know that I am your friend."

"I think indeed that you are my friend," Othello said. "And since I know that you are full of friendship and honesty, and that you carefully consider your words before you speak them, these sudden pauses of yours frighten me all the more. Such things in a false disloyal knave are tricks of a dishonest trade, but in a man who is just and fair they are expressions of hidden thoughts that come from the heart and that emotions cannot control."

"I dare to swear that I think that Cassio is honest and trustworthy."

"I dare to swear the same thing," Othello said.

"Men should be what they seem to be," Iago said. "I wish that men who are not honest would be seen and known to be not honest."

"Certainly, men should be what they seem," Othello said.

"Why, then, I think Cassio is an honest man," Iago said.

"You are not telling me everything you are thinking," Othello said. "Please, tell me what you think. Obviously, you suspect something. Give the worst of your thoughts the worst of words."

"My good lord, pardon me," Iago replied. "Though I am bound to every act of duty, I am not bound to do that which all slaves are free not to do. Utter my thoughts? Why, let's say that my thoughts are vile and false; after all, where is that palace into which foul things never intrude? Who has a breast so pure that no unclean thoughts and ideas ever appear and sit beside pure thoughts and ideas?"

"You conspire against your friend, Iago, if you think that he has been wronged and you never tell him what you think."

"Please do not make me tell you what I am thinking. Chances are, what I am thinking is wrong. It is a fault of my character to inquire into evils, and often my suspicions are about evils that turn out not to exist. I ask you not to take any notice of my suspicions, which often turn out to be wrong; do not bring yourself trouble because of my casual and unsure observations. It will disrupt your calm and quiet life and will not be good for you. Not for my manhood, honesty, or wisdom would I let you know my thoughts."

"What do you mean?"

"The good name and reputation of man and woman, my dear lord, is the most precious jewel of their souls," Iago said. "Who steals my money steals trash; it is something trivial. It was mine, now it is his, and it has been the servant of thousands of people. But he who steals from me my good name robs me of something that does not enrich him but makes me poor indeed."

"By Heaven, I will know what you are thinking."

"You cannot — not even if my heart were in your hand," Iago said, "and you shall not, while my heart is in my custody."

"We will see about that," Othello said.

"Beware, my lord, of jealousy, which is traditionally associated with the color green," Iago replied. "Jealousy is a green-eyed monster that mocks and torments its victim. A man who is sure that his wife has made him a cuckold by sleeping with another man lives in bliss when he does not love the wife who cuckolded him. But damned are the minutes of a man who loves his wife but doubts her and suspects her and still strongly loves her!"

"Such a life would be miserable," Othello said.

"A man who is poor but is happy despite being poor is a rich man indeed," Iago said, "but a man with unlimited wealth is as poor as winter if he always is afraid that he may become poor. Good Heaven, may the spirits of all my ancestors protect me from jealousy!"

"Why are you saying these things?" Othello asked. "Do you think that I would live a life of jealousy and have new suspicions with each change of the Moon? No. To be once in doubt is to resolve on a course of action — one can form a plan of action to find out whether the doubt is justified. If I should ever turn the business of my soul to such exaggerated and inflated surmises that match what you are implying, then I will be a goat. It is not enough to make me jealous to say that my wife is beautiful, is good company during meals, loves the company of other people, speaks interestingly, and sings, plays musical instruments, and dances well. When a woman has virtue, such abilities increase her virtue. Nor from my own weak merits will I draw the smallest fear or doubt about her fidelity. When she was single, she saw clearly with her eyes, and she chose to marry me. No, Iago. I will have to see evidence before I doubt her fidelity; when I doubt her fidelity, I will seek proof either that she is faithful or that she is not faithful. On the basis of that proof, I will either cease loving her or stop being jealous of her!"

"I am glad of it," Iago replied, "because now I have reason to show you openly the love and duty that I owe you; therefore, as I am bound to speak the truth, hear it from me. I am not speaking yet of proof. Watch your wife; observe her carefully when she is with Cassio. Watch with an open mind. Do not let your eyes be biased either by jealousy or by overconfidence that your wife is faithful. I do not want you to be hurt by falsely assuming that because you are honest and trustworthy, other people are also honest and trustworthy. Be careful. I know the people of Venice. In Venice, wives are willing to let Heaven see the sins that they dare not show their husbands. Their consciences do not tell them not to sin, but instead to keep the sin hidden."

"Do you truly believe that?" Othello asked.

"Desdemona deceived her father when she eloped with you without first getting his permission, and when she seemed to tremble and fear your looks to deceive her father, that is when she loved you most. Remember what her father told you: 'Watch her carefully, Moor,' Brabantio said, 'if you have eyes to use. She has deceived her father, and she may deceive you.'"

"She did deceive her father," Othello said.

"Why, there you are," Iago said. "She is one who, despite being so young, could act and deceive her father so well that it was as if he were blind — her father even thought that you had manipulated her with witchcraft. But I am much to blame for telling you this. I humbly do beg your pardon that I have spoken so freely because I respect you so much."

"I am forever in your debt," Othello said.

"I see that this has dampened your spirits a little."

Othello lied, "Not at all. Not at all."

"I am afraid that it has," Iago replied. "I hope that you know that I have spoken these things because of my concern for you. But I can see that you're affected by what I have said. Please do not overanalyze what I have said and jump to conclusions — just be suspicious."

"I won't jump to conclusions."

"Should you do so, my lord, my speech could have a vile effect. I did not intend that. Cassio is my worthy friend — my lord, I see you're upset."

"No, not very upset," Othello said. "I do not think anything except that Desdemona is faithful to me."

"May she live long and be faithful to you!" Iago said. "And may you live long and think that she is faithful to you!"

"Yet," Othello said, "a person may turn away from one's true nature."

"Yes, that's the point!" Iago said. "If I may be blunt with you, a woman sometimes does not want a marriage — even if she has had many marriage proposals of this kind — with a man from her own climate, of her own color, and from her own social standing. Yet that is the kind of marriage that our nature inclines us toward. In rejecting such a marriage, such a woman's use of her free will shows itself to be most rank. She engages in foul impropriety and indulges her unnatural thoughts.

"But pardon me; I do not positively and specifically speak about Desdemona, although I fear that she, returning to her better judgment, may begin to compare you with her fellow countrymen and perhaps may repent having married you."

"Farewell, farewell," Othello said. "If you see anything more, let me know. Also, tell your wife to watch Desdemona. Leave me now, Iago."

"My lord, I take my leave."

Iago walked away.

Othello thought, *Why did I get married? This honest man — Iago — doubtless sees and knows more, much more, than he has told me.*

Iago returned and said, "My lord, I wish to ask your honor to consider this matter no further. Wait and see what happens. Although it is fitting that Cassio be reinstated as your lieutenant, because indeed he does his job with great ability, yet if you are willing not to reinstate him for a while, you will be able to watch him and see how he responds. See whether your wife strongly or vehemently urges that he be reinstated. That will tell you much. In the meantime, think that I am overreacting to my fears — although I think I have worthy reasons for my fears — and please consider her to be innocent."

"You need not fear my self-control," Othello replied.

"I once more take my leave."

Iago departed.

"Iago is a man of great honesty," Othello said to himself. "He understands different kinds of people and how and why they act as they do. If I discover proof that Desdemona is wild and untamed and not like a civilized and obedient wife, I will — even though the ties that bind her to me are my own heartstrings — cast her aside and let her be wild and untamed and take care of herself. Perhaps, because I am black and do not converse as well as courtiers and ladies' men, or because I am older than she is — yet I am not that old — she has not been faithful to me. I am and have been deceived, and my relief must be to hate her. It is the curse of marriage that we can call these delicate creatures ours, and yet their desires are not ours! I would prefer to be a loathsome toad and live in the foul air of a dungeon than allow the pudendum of my wife to be used by other men. Yet, this is the plague of great men; they are less likely than less important men to have faithful wives because their duties keep them so often and so long away from home. This is a destiny that cannot be avoided, like death. The fate of a cuckold is ours even from the time we begin to move in our mother's womb."

He looked up and said to himself, "I see Desdemona coming now. If she is unfaithful to me, then Heaven is mocking itself by creating a woman who is so beautiful and yet is unfaithful — I will not believe that Heaven has done such a thing."

Desdemona and Emilia walked over to Othello.

Desdemona asked, "How are you, my dear Othello! Your dinner and the generous islanders whom you have invited to eat with us are waiting for your arrival."

"My lateness is my fault," Othello replied.

"Why do you speak so faintly?" Desdemona asked. "Are you not well?"

"I have a pain on my forehead here," Othello said, pointing to where the horns of a cuckold were supposed to grow.

"Your headache is caused by a lack of sleep," Desdemona said. "It will go away. Let me tie your head with my handkerchief, and within an hour your headache will vanish."

"Your handkerchief is too small," Othello said, pushing it away.

The handkerchief fell to the ground.

Othello said, "You need not bind my head. Come, I will go in to dinner with you."

"I am very sorry that you are not well," Desdemona said. Because she was so concerned about her husband's not feeling well, she did not think about her handkerchief.

She and Othello left to go to dinner, leaving the handkerchief on the ground.

Emilia picked up the handkerchief and said, "I am glad I have found this handkerchief. This was the first keepsake the Moor gave her. My headstrong husband has a hundred times urged me to steal it, but she loves the love-token. Her husband made her swear to keep it forever, and she keeps it always with her so that she can kiss it and talk to it. I'll have the embroidery — a pattern of strawberries that is a work of art — copied onto another handkerchief and give it to my husband, Iago. What he will do with it, Heaven knows and not I. I want nothing except to gratify his whim."

Iago appeared and said to Emilia, "How are you? What are you doing here alone?"

"Don't rebuke me. I have a thing for you."

"A thing for me? It is a common thing —"

Iago and Emilia did not always get along. Iago now seemed to be insulting his wife. Nowadays, "thing" refers to a penis, but in Iago's country and day, "thing" referred to both male and female genitalia. To say that Emilia's thing was common meant that her thing was open to all.

Shocked, Emilia said, "What!"

And Iago concluded, "— to have a foolish wife."

Emilia said, "Is that all? I was expecting a much worse insult."

Wanting to keep on her husband's good side — he could be especially mean when she was not on his good side — Emilia said, "What will you say to me now if I give you a handkerchief?"

"What handkerchief?"

"What handkerchief? Why, the handkerchief that the Moor first gave to Desdemona — the handkerchief that so often you have asked me to steal."

"Did you steal it from her?"

"No. She negligently let it drop to the ground. I was lucky enough to be present and picked it up."

"Good girl," Iago said. "Give it to me."

"What will you do with it? Why have you been so eager for me to steal it?"

Iago snatched the handkerchief away from his wife and said, "What business is that of yours?"

"If you don't need it for something important," Emilia said, "give it back to me. Poor Desdemona will be very upset when she discovers that she has lost it."

"Pretend that you know nothing about this handkerchief. I need it. Go, now, leave me."

Emilia departed.

Iago thought, *I will plant this handkerchief in Cassio's lodging and let him find it. Trifles light as air are to the jealous confirmations as strong as the proofs found in holy scripture. This handkerchief will advance my plot. The Moor is already changing with my poisonous words: Dangerous thoughts are, in their nature, poison. At first, the poisonous words seem to have little effect, then the poison spreads and infects one's whole being. The poisonous thoughts burn like sulfur mines. I say this because I know this.*

Iago looked up and saw Othello walking toward him.

Iago thought, *Already my poison is working. Opium and other soporifics will never again give the Moor the sweet sleep that he enjoyed as recently as yesterday.*

Othello was mumbling to himself, "Has she been unfaithful to me? Has she cheated on me?"

"How are you, general?" Iago said. "Please, torment yourself no longer with jealousy."

"Go away!" Othello said. "Leave! Your words have put me on the rack and are torturing me. I swear that it is better to be cheated on continuously and not know it than to be cheated on a little and know it."

"What do you mean, my lord?" Iago asked.

"What did I know about her stolen hours of lust? I did not see them, I did not think about them, they did not harm me. Each time she was unfaithful, I slept well the following night and I was free of jealousy and I was happy. I was not aware of Cassio's kisses on her lips. A man who was robbed, but does not know he was robbed, has not been robbed at all."

"I am sorry to hear this," Iago said.

"I would be happy, if all the soldiers of the camp, including the very lowest in rank, had tasted her sweet body, as long as I was not aware of it," Othello said. "But now, my tranquil mind is gone forever. Farewell, tranquility! Farewell, happiness! And farewell to my career! Farewell to the troops! Farewell to the big wars that turn ambition into a virtue! Farewell to the neighing steeds, and the shrill trumpets, the spirit-stirring drums, the ear-piercing fifes, the royal banners, and all attributes, proud display, pomp, and ceremonies of glorious war! All you deadly cannon whose rude throats counterfeit the deadly thunder and lightning of immortal Jove, farewell! My career is over!"

"Can that be possible, my lord?" Iago asked.

"Villain, make sure that you prove my wife is a whore," Othello said. "Make sure of it. Give me proof that I can see with my eyes, or I swear by my immortal soul that it would have been better for you to be born a dog than to face my awakened wrath!"

"Has it come to this?"

"Show me proof, or, at the least, so prove that my wife is a whore that the proof will have nowhere on which a doubt can hang — or you will lose your life!"

"My noble lord —"

"If you are slandering her and torturing me, do not bother to pray and abandon all repentance for your sins. Horrors accumulate on the head of a man who is horrible. Do deeds so evil that they will make Heaven weep and amaze everybody on Earth because you can do nothing that can add more to your damnation than what you have already done!"

"May the grace of God and Heaven forgive me for being so honest," Iago said. "Are you a man? Do you have a soul or sense? May God be with you. I resign my office — make someone else your ancient. I am a wretched fool because I have lived to see that my honesty is considered a vice! Oh, monstrous world! Take note, people, take note: To be direct and honest is not safe. I thank you for this wisdom I have learned, and from here on I will have no friends because making friends leads to abuse from those so-called friends."

Iago started to walk away.

Othello said, "Stay. You ought to be honest."

"I ought to be wise," Iago replied. "An honest man is a fool who loses the friends he tries to help."

"I would bet the world that my wife is faithful to me, and yet I think that she is not. I think that you are just and yet I think that you are not. I need some proof. My wife's name, that was as fresh and clean as the face of the virgin goddess Diana, is now as begrimed and black as my own face. If ropes, or knives, or poison, or fire, or suffocating streams, exist, I will not endure it."

Iago thought, *Are you thinking about killing Desdemona and Cassio — or yourself? I am OK with either decision.*

"I wish I knew the truth for certain!" Othello said.

"I see, sir, that you are eaten up with suffering," Iago said. "I am sorry that I told you what I suspect. But do you really want to know the truth?"

"I do want to know the truth — and I *will* know the truth!"

"And you shall know the truth," Iago said. "But how? How can we get you the proof you need? Would you have to catch her in the act of betraying you? Would you have to see her in bed with a man on top of her?"

"Death and damnation!" Othello exclaimed.

"It would be difficult, I think, to catch your wife and her lover in the act of betraying you," Iago said. "Damn them if ever mortal eyes other than their own see them go to bed together! So what can we do? How can we get proof? How can your need for proof be satisfied? It is impossible for you to see them in bed together. They will take precautions even if they are as lecherous as goats, as horny as monkeys, as lustful as wolves in heat, and as foolish as stupid, drunken people. But still, I say, if rational inferences and strong circumstantial evidence that together lead directly to the door of truth will give you satisfactory evidence, you may have your proof."

"Give me valid evidence that she is disloyal to me."

"I do not like this job you are giving to me," Iago said. "But, since I am already involved in this situation because of my foolish honesty and respect for you, I will go on. As you know, in our culture, it is acceptable for two people of the same sex to share a bed. I lay beside Cassio recently. Because I was troubled with a raging toothache, I could not sleep. Some men are so indiscrete that when they are asleep they will mutter about their affairs. Cassio is such a man. As he lay asleep, I heard him say, 'Sweet Desdemona, let us be wary. Let us hide our love for each other.' And then, sir, he gripped and wrung my hand, cried, 'Sweetheart!' and kissed me hard, as if he were plucking up kisses by the roots that grew upon my lips. He then laid his leg over my thigh, and sighed, and kissed, and then he cried, 'Cursed be the fate that gave you to the Moor!'"

The Moor is likely to believe this lie, Iago thought.

"Oh, monstrous! Monstrous!" Othello said.

"This was only his dream."

"But this is evidence of a previous coupling," Othello said. "Cassio's dream is circumstantial evidence that he is having an affair with my wife."

"This dream may serve to bolster other evidence that only weakly points to an affair."

"I will tear her to pieces!" Othello cried.

"Don't," Iago said. "But be wise. So far, we have no visual evidence. We may yet find out that your wife is faithful to you. But tell me, doesn't your wife own an expensive handkerchief that is embroidered with a pattern of strawberries?"

"I gave her that handkerchief," Othello said. "It was my first gift to her."

"I did not know that," Iago said. "But I saw today Cassio wiping his beard with that handkerchief — I am sure that it is your wife's."

"If that was the handkerchief I gave her —"

"If it was, or if it was any handkerchief that belonged to her, it is yet more evidence that she is unfaithful to you."

"I wish that this slave — Cassio — had forty thousand lives! One is not enough for me to give adequate expression to my rage. I know now that he is having an affair with my wife! Iago, listen. All the foolish love I had for my wife I now blow up to Heaven — that love is gone. Arise, black vengeance, from your home in hollow Hell! My love for Desdemona, leave my mind and heart and give up your place to tyrannous hatred! Swell, mind and heart, with your burden, which is the venom of poisonous snakes!"

"Calm down," Iago advised.

"I want blood!" Othello said. "Blood! Blood! Blood!"

"Be patient and wait a while," Iago said. "You may change your mind."

"Never, Iago," Othello replied. "My bloody thoughts are like the current of the Black Sea, which always flows strongly to the Mediterranean Sea. Because water always flows from a higher to a lower elevation, the current never flows from the Mediterranean Sea to the Black Sea. Similarly, my bloody thoughts shall never look backward toward a humble love but shall always violently rush forward toward a suitable and all-encompassing revenge."

Othello knelt and said, "I swear a sacred vow by Heaven, which is shining and changeless, that I will get revenge."

Iago said, "Do not rise yet."

He knelt beside Othello and made his own vow: "Witness, you ever-burning lights above, you elements that encircle us, that here Iago gives up the control of his mind, hands, and heart to Othello — Iago will follow the orders of Othello, who has been wronged by his wife. Let him command me to do anything at all, and I will do whatever bloody business he orders me to do as if I were doing a good deed. I will feel no remorse but instead shall value serving Othello."

They rose.

Othello said, "I will acknowledge your service to me not with empty thanks, but with profit to you. Immediately, I ask you to keep your vow: Within three days bring it about that I will hear that Cassio no longer lives."

"Cassio, who is my friend, will die," Iago said. "I will kill him as you request, but let Desdemona continue to live."

"Damn her, that lewd and wanton whore! Damn her! Come with me. I will go inside and equip myself with some means to swiftly kill that beautiful devil. You are now my lieutenant."

"I am yours to command forever."

Desdemona and Emilia were standing on a street in front of the castle. Also on the street was a man whom Desdemona recognized; he was a clown, aka Fool, aka comedian. Desdemona knew that he played with language, and because she was worried about her handkerchief, which had turned up missing, she decided to speak to the clown: "Do you know, please, where Lieutenant Cassio lies?"

In. this culture, to ask where a person lies meant. To ask where a person resided — that is, slept.

"Why not, man?"

"Cassio is a soldier, and when a person says that a soldier lies, that person is in for a stabbing."

Being called a liar was a major insult. They were fighting words.

Desdemona laughed and then said, "Where does he lodge? Where does he dwell?"

"To tell you where he lodges is to tell you where I lie."

"Can any sense be made of what you just said?"

"I do not know where he lodges, and for me to make up a lodging and say that he lies here or that he lies there would be to lie in my own throat."

"Can you inquire about him, and be edified by report?"

"To be edified is to be educated; therefore, I will catechize the world for him; that is, I will ask questions, listen to the answers, and so learn where he is, and then I will bring the information to you."

"Seek him, find him, and tell him to come here," Desdemona said. "Tell him that I have talked to my lord and husband on his behalf, and I hope that all will be well."

"To do this is within the scope of a man's intelligence, and therefore I will attempt the doing of it."

The clown departed.

Desdemona asked, "Where could I have lost that handkerchief, Emilia?"

Emilia lied, "I don't know, Madam."

"Believe me, I prefer to have lost a purse full of gold coins marked with the Christian cross. Fortunately, my noble Moor is true of mind and trusts me and is not like a base and jealous man. If he were not, my losing that handkerchief could make him think badly of me."

"Isn't he jealous?" Emilia, whose husband was jealous, asked.

"Who? Othello?" Desdemona replied. "I think that he was born without a jealous atom in his body."

"Look, here he comes," Emilia said.

"I will not leave him until he promises to make Cassio his lieutenant again," Desdemona said. "This is a good opportunity for me to act in behalf of Cassio. I expect to give Cassio good news when he arrives."

Othello walked up to them.

"How are you, my lord?" Desdemona asked.

"I am well, my good lady," Othello said.

It is hard to pretend that I am well, he thought. *I am far from being well.*

"How are you, Desdemona?" he asked.

"Well, my good lord," she replied.

"Give me your hand," Othello said. He held it and said, "This hand is moist, my lady."

Othello thought, *A moist hand is evidence of a lustful nature.*

"My hand has of yet felt no age nor sorrow."

She thought, *A moist hand is evidence of a youthful and carefree nature.*

"A moist hand is evidence of fruitfulness and a liberal heart," Othello said.

He thought, *The word "liberal" means either "generous" or "licentious."*

"Your hand is hot — hot and moist," he added. "Based on these symptoms, this hand of yours requires less liberty, much fasting and prayer, much corrective discipline, and many religious observances. Here is a young and sweating devil, and that kind of devil commonly rebels. But it is a good hand because it is a frank hand."

To be frank is to be generous or to be open and free from restraint, Othello thought. *People should appear to be what they really are. Desdemona's hand is good because it frankly — openly and freely — reveals what she really is: lustful.*

"You may, indeed, say that my hand is generous," Desdemona replied, "because that hand gave away my heart."

Desdemona meant that her hand gave away her heart to Othello.

"Your hand is a liberal hand," Othello said, meaning that her hand had given away her heart to men other than him.

He added, "The hearts of old gave hands, but our new heraldry is hands, not hearts."

He thought, *People used to give away their heart and hands to one person, but nowadays the fashion is to give away one's hand in marriage to one person and one's loving heart to another person. Hearts, united in love, used to give away hands in marriage, but nowadays, hands, despite belonging to a married person, give away hearts to people to whom they are not married.*

"I don't know about that," Desdemona said. "But come now, remember your promise."

"What promise, darling?"

"I have sent a messenger to ask Cassio to come and speak with you."

"I have an irritating and constant cold that is bothering me," Othello replied. "Lend me your handkerchief."

"Here, my lord," Desdemona replied, handing him a handkerchief.

"Not that one. Give me the one I gave you."

"I don't have it with me."

"You don't?"

"No, indeed, my lord."

"That's too bad," Othello said. "An Egyptian gave that handkerchief to my mother. The Egyptian was a magician who used charms and spells; she could almost read people's minds. She told my mother that as long as she had that handkerchief, it would make her beloved and keep my father in love with her, but if she lost it or gave it away, my father would hate the sight of her and he would chase other women. On her deathbed, my mother gave it to me and told me that when I married to give it to my wife. I did so. Take care of it and regard it as precious as your own eyes. To lose it or give it away would cause such damage that nothing could match it."

"Is that really true?" Desdemona asked.

"It is true," Othello said. "When the Egyptian wove it, she wove magic into the cloth. A Sibyl in her prophetic fury sewed the handkerchief. Some say that the Sybil was two hundred years old; others say that she had calculated that the world would end in two hundred years. But the worms were consecrated that produced the silk, and it was dyed in the liquid called mummy — medicinal fluid that skillful magicians had made from the liquid of the hearts of embalmed virgins."

"Really! And is that true?"

"It is very true," Othello replied. "Therefore, take good care of that handkerchief."

"If what you said is true, then I wish to God that I had never seen that handkerchief!"

"Why?" Othello shouted.

"Why do you speak so abruptly and urgently?" Desdemona asked.

"Is it lost? Is it gone? Speak! Is it missing?"

"Heaven bless us!" Desdemona said, startled by Othello's urgency.

"What do you say?"

"It is not lost," Desdemona said.

I think that my handkerchief is not forever lost, Desdemona thought. *I must have mislaid it somewhere, and it will turn up again.*

"But what if the handkerchief were lost?" she asked.

"What!"

"I say again that the handkerchief is not lost."

"Go and fetch it. Let me see it."

"Why, I could do that, sir, but I will not now. This is a trick that you are playing to distract me from asking you to reinstate Cassio as your lieutenant. Please, reinstate him."

"Fetch the handkerchief for me. I don't think that you are telling me the truth."

"Come, come. You'll never meet a man more competent than Cassio."

"The handkerchief!"

"Please, let us talk about Cassio."

"The handkerchief!"

"Cassio is a man who has counted on your support for his good fortune. He has shared dangers with you —"

"The handkerchief!"

"Truly, you are to blame."

"That's enough!" Othello shouted and then stalked away.

"You said that he is not jealous?" Emilia asked.

"I have never seen him like this before," Desdemona said. "Surely, there really is some wonderful magic in that handkerchief. I am very unhappy because of the loss of it."

"It takes more than a year or two to learn a man's true nature," said Emilia, whose marriage to Iago was not happy. "Men are nothing but stomachs, and we women are nothing but food. They eat us hungrily and then vomit us up."

She looked up and said, "Look, Cassio and my husband are coming!"

Cassio and Iago had been conversing, and Iago said now, "There is no other way; it is she who must do it."

He looked up and added, "Look, happily she is here! Go, and ask her."

"How are you, good Cassio! What is the news with you?" Desdemona asked.

"Madam, I have come to talk with you about my former lieutenancy," Cassio said. "I beg you to do all you can to help me get my life back and be on good terms again with your husband. I greatly respect him, and I don't want to wait any longer. If my offence is of such a serious kind that my past services, nor the repentance I have now for what I did wrong, nor the service that I can render to him in the future, can make him forgive me, I want to know it now. My benefit will be to know the truth so that I can force myself to move on and hope that I have the good fortune to find another occupation."

"I am sorry, thrice-gentle Cassio," Desdemona said, "but I am unable to help you at this time. My lord and husband is not acting like my lord and husband. I would not be able to recognize him if his face were as altered as his personality. I swear to every sanctified spirit that I have pleaded your case to the best of my ability — because I have spoken so freely, I am suffering from my husband's displeasure. You must be patient for a while longer. I will do what I can for you, and I will do more for you than I dare to do for myself. Let that satisfy you for now."

"Is the general angry?" Iago asked.

"He left just now," Emilia said, "and he was greatly upset."

"I did not know it was possible for him to be angry," Iago said. "I have seen cannon blow Othello's soldiers into the air and like the devil kill Othello's brother while his brother was standing by his side, yet he showed no emotion — and *now* he is angry? Something of great importance has occurred. I will go and talk to him. If he is angry, it is about something of great importance."

"Please, go and talk to him," Desdemona replied.

Iago departed.

She added, "Iago must be right. Some great affair of state — something that concerns Venice or a plot in Cyprus that he has just learned about — must have disturbed and muddied his mind. In such cases, men will argue about unimportant things although great, important matters are on their minds. It is often like that. If only one finger aches, it negatively affects our whole body and mind even though they are healthy. We must remember that men are only mortal — they are not gods. At such times, we must not expect men to act as they did during the marriage ceremony. I am at fault, Emilia. I was, unskillful 'warrior' as I am, accusing him in my soul of being unkind, but now I find that I have caused the witness — myself — to lie by misinterpreting Othello's behavior. I have unfairly accused Othello."

"Pray to Heaven that it is matters of state, as you think, that cause Othello to act this way," Emilia said, "and not a misconception that is causing him to be jealous concerning you."

"I have never given him any reason to be jealous," Desdemona said.

"But jealous souls will not care about that," Emilia said. "They are not jealous because they have a just reason to be jealous. No, instead they are jealous because they are jealous. Jealousy is a monster that gives birth to itself; it does not need a reason to come into existence."

"May Heaven keep that monster from Othello's mind!" Desdemona said.

"Lady, amen to that!" Emilia said.

"I will go and seek him," Desdemona said. "Cassio, stay here. If I find Othello in a better mood, I will plead that you regain your lieutenancy."

"I humbly thank your ladyship," Cassio said.

Desdemona and Emilia left to seek Othello.

Bianca, who had been looking for Cassio, now walked up to him. She was a prostitute, and she loved Cassio, but he did not return her love although he slept with her.

"May God save you, friend Cassio!" Bianca said.

"What are you doing away from home? How are you, my most beautiful Bianca? Truly, sweet love, I was coming to your house."

"And I was going to your lodging, Cassio," Bianca replied. "You have not visited me for a week! Seven days and nights! Eight score and eight hours! When lovers are away from each other, each hour lasts eight score times longer than it usually does! Such arithmetic is disheartening."

"Pardon me, Bianca, for my absence," Cassio said. "I have this past week been burdened with heavy problems, but I shall, in a time less burdened and interrupted with problems, make my long absence up to you. Sweet Bianca, I want you to do something for me."

He handed Desdemona's handkerchief to her and said, "Please copy this embroidery."

"Cassio, where did this come from?" Bianca asked. "This is some keepsake from a new lover. Now I know why I have not seen you for so long. Has it come to this?"

"No, woman!" Cassio said. "Throw your vile suppositions back in the devil's teeth from whence you got them. You are jealous now because you think that this is a keepsake from some woman. No. I swear that it is not, Bianca."

"Why, then whose handkerchief is it?"

"I don't know, sweetheart. I found it in my bedchamber. I like the embroidery well — it is a pattern of strawberries. I expect that its owner will show up and want it back — that is likely to happen. But before it happens, I would like to have it copied. Take the handkerchief, and copy the embroidery onto another handkerchief, and leave me for a while."

"Leave you for a while! Why?"

"I am waiting here to speak to the general," Cassio said. "I do not think it will help my cause if I have a woman with me during this serious business."

"Why don't you want me here?"

"It is not that I don't love you."

"You don't love me," Bianca said petulantly. Then she relented and said, "Please walk with me for a little while as I return home and please tell me whether I will see you soon one night."

"I can walk with you for only a little way because I have important business here," Cassio said, "but I will see you soon."

"Very well," Bianca said. "I must be happy with what I can get."

CHAPTER 4

— 4.1 —

Othello and Iago were speaking in front of the castle.

"Do you think that?" Iago asked.

"Think what?" Othello asked.

"That they kissed in private?"

"An unauthorized, illicit kiss!"

"Do you think that it is possible she was naked with her friend in bed for an hour or more, not meaning any harm?"

"Naked in bed, Iago, and not mean harm!" Othello thundered. "That would be hypocrisy against the devil. Those who seem to be acting sinfully and yet are virtuous in their heart are people whom the devil would call hypocrites. If they did act like that, they would be setting themselves up for the devil to tempt them, and they would be tempting Heaven to damn them."

"As long as they are naked in bed together and do not commit adultery, it is a venial slip — less serious than a venial sin, which is a sin that can be forgiven," Iago said, "but if I give my wife a handkerchief —"

He paused.

"What then?" Othello asked.

"Why, then, the handkerchief belongs to her, my lord, and since it belongs to her, she can give it to any man she pleases."

"Her honor belongs to her, too," Othello said. "Does it follow that she can give that away, too?"

"Her honor is an essence that cannot be seen. Women very often have a reputation for honor although they lack honor. But, as for the handkerchief —"

"By Heaven, I would very gladly forget about the handkerchief. Now that I know — because you told me — that Cassio has it, each time I remember it, it affects me like a raven on the roof of a house that has been infected with the plague. It is an evil omen of death and doom to all who see it or know that it is there."

"It is true that I told you that."

"That was bad news for me."

"Suppose that I have more bad news for you," Iago said. "Suppose I say that I have seen Cassio do you wrong? Or suppose that I have heard Cassio say — you know, of course, that adulterers exist in the world who have seduced and overcome a woman or been seduced by a willing woman and in either case have been sexually satisfied and have been eager to blab —"

Othello interrupted, "Has Cassio said anything?"

"He has, my lord, but be assured that he will deny that he ever said anything."

"What has he said?"

"Truly, he said that —"

Iago hesitated, and then he said, "I don't know what he said."

"He said something so horrible that you don't want to tell me what he said, but tell me anyway."

"He talked about lying —"

Again, Iago hesitated.

"Lying with her?" Othello said.

"With her. On her. Whatever," Iago replied.

"Lying with her? Lying on her? I would prefer that people lie about her than lie on top of her — adultery is disgusting! I have the evidence of the handkerchief and this verbal confession. My handkerchief! He has confessed, and he should be hanged for what he did! I am willing to hang him first and allow him to confess his sins after he is dead. I am so angry that I am trembling. It would not be natural for me to feel this way and to tremble in this way unless there was a good reason to do so. It is not merely words that make me tremble like this. No! I will cut off their noses, ears, and lips! Can all this really be true? He confessed, and he has my handkerchief — damn!"

Othello fell down in an epileptic fit.

Work on, my "medicine," work on! Iago thought. *In this way credulous fools are caught, and in this way many worthy and chaste women meet reproach although they are guiltless.*

Seeing Cassio coming, Iago put on an act for his benefit. Iago pretended to be concerned about Othello and said loudly enough for Cassio to hear, "My lord, wake up! Othello!"

He looked up and said, "Cassio!"

"What's the matter?"

"My lord is having another epileptic fit. This is his second fit; he had one yesterday."

"Rub his temples."

"No, we better not," Iago said. "His unconsciousness must run its course. If it does not, he foams at the mouth and then breaks out in a savage madness. Look, he is regaining consciousness. Go away for a little while. He will recover quickly. After he leaves, I want to talk to you about something important."

Cassio departed, and Othello regained consciousness.

"How are you, general? Does your head hurt?"

"Are you making fun of me?" Othello said angrily, thinking that Iago was saying that his head hurt because he was growing the horns of a cuckold.

"Making fun of you? No, but by God, I wish that you would bear your ill fortune like a man!"

"A horned man is a monster and a beast."

"In that case, there is many a beast in a populous city, and many a civilized monster."

"Did Cassio confess?"

"Good sir, be a man," Iago said. "You should think that every mature man who has been married — yoked like a horned beast to pull a burden — has the same burden as you. Millions of men are now alive who each night lie in beds that they think belong only to them but which they share with their wife's lovers. Your situation is better than theirs: You know that your wife is unfaithful. The malice of Hell — the worst mockery — is to kiss a wanton whore on a bed that the husband thinks is his alone. No, I prefer to know that I have been cuckolded. Knowing that, I know what revenge to take on my wife."

"Certainly, you are a wise man," Othello said.

"Stand for a while at a little distance," Iago said, "and control yourself. While you were overwhelmed with your suffering and had fallen into a fit — grief most unsuitable for such a man as you — Cassio came here. I came up with an excuse to get him to go away and made a good excuse for your falling into a fit. I also asked him to return here and speak to me, which he promised to do. Therefore, conceal yourself and witness the sneers, the mockery, and the obvious contempt that can be seen in every region of his face. You can witness these things because I will make him tell the story again of where, how, how often, how long ago, and when he has slept — and will again sleep — with your wife. Watch his gestures carefully. But be patient and do not reveal yourself, or I shall say you are consumed with passion and ruled by anger and are not a real man."

Iago thought, *If Othello were to actually talk to Cassio, he would learn how I have been tricking him.*

"Listen to me, Iago," Othello replied. "I will control myself, but I will have blood — lots of blood."

"There is nothing wrong with that," Iago said, "but make those who have wronged you bleed at the right time. Will you conceal yourself nearby and watch as I talk with Cassio?"

Othello walked a short distance away and hid himself.

Iago thought, *Now I will ask Cassio questions about Bianca, the whore who loves him — by selling her body she is able to buy herself food and clothing. She loves Cassio — prostitutes seduce many men but are often themselves seduced by one man. Cassio does not love her. When he hears about her and her love for him, he cannot stop himself from laughing. Here comes Cassio now. Cassio shall smile and laugh, and Othello shall go insane. The Moor's ignorant jealousy will interpret Cassio's smiles, gestures, and cheerful behavior completely the wrong way. He will not be able to hear our words; he will only be able to see our gestures and hear Cassio's laughter.*

Cassio walked up to Iago, who asked, "How are you, lieutenant?"

"I feel worse because you have called me by a title I don't have anymore — the lack of that title is killing me."

"Keep pushing Desdemona to help you, and you are sure to regain your lieutenancy."

Iago lowered his voice and said, "Suppose that Bianca were able to plead your case. How quickly would you become lieutenant then!"

Cassio laughed and said, "That poor woman."

Othello thought, *Already he is laughing!*

Iago said, "I have never known a woman to so love a man."

"That poor rogue!" Cassio said. "I think, indeed, that she loves me."

Othello thought, *Now he is faintly denying the affair, and he is laughing about it.*

"Listen to me, Cassio," Iago said.

Othello thought, *Now Iago is asking Cassio to tell him about his affair with my wife. Well done, Iago.*

"Bianca is telling everyone that you will marry her," Iago said. "Will you really marry her?"

Cassio laughed loudly.

Othello thought, *Are you laughing about triumphing over me like a Roman conqueror?*

"I marry her!" Cassio said. "Please, give me credit for some intelligence — don't think that I am stupid enough to marry a whore."

You are laughing now, Othello thought, *but it is better to be the last one who laughs.*

"Indeed, the gossip is everywhere that you will marry her."

"Tell me the truth."

"This is truly what people are saying — or else I am a villain."

Have you wounded me? Othello thought. *Just wait.*

"That is the monkey's own story. She is persuaded that I will marry her because of her own love for me and because of her belief that I love her. I have never told her that I will marry her."

Iago gestured to Othello to come closer, and Othello thought, *Now Cassio is going to tell the tale of his affair with my wife.*

Cassio said, "She was here just now; she haunts me in every place. Just the other day I was talking on the seashore with some people from Venice, and here she — this plaything — comes and throws her arms around my neck."

Othello thought, *Desdemona must have hugged him and called him "dear Cassio"! That is what his gesture means.*

Laughing, Cassio said, "She had her arms around my neck, and hung from me, and cried. She tugged at me and pulled me."

Othello thought, *Now he is telling how Desdemona pulled him into my bedchamber. I can see your nose, Cassio, but I cannot see the dog that I will throw it to after I have cut it off.*

"Well, after hearing what you have told me," Cassio said, "I must stop seeing her."

"Look!" Iago said. "Bianca is walking toward us!"

"She is a polecat," Cassio said to Iago. "They stink when they are in heat. Bianca drenches herself in perfume."

He said to Bianca, "What do you mean by this haunting of me? Why are you following me everywhere?"

"Let the devil and his dam haunt you!" Bianca replied.

"What did you mean by that embroidered handkerchief you gave me just now? I was a fine fool to take it. You want me to copy the embroidery? You told me quite a tale — you found it in your bedchamber and you don't know how it got there! A likely story! This is a keepsake from some slut. Take it — give it to your slut. Wherever you got this handkerchief, I will not copy the embroidery."

"Sweet Bianca, don't be upset," Cassio said.

Othello thought, *That's my handkerchief!*

Bianca said to Cassio, "If you want to eat supper at my place tonight, you may. If you don't come tonight, then come the next time I prepare a meal for you — that will be never."

She left.

"Go after her," Iago urged Cassio.

"I had better," Cassio said. "She will scream complaints about me in the streets if I don't."

"Will you dine with her?" Iago asked.

"Yes."

"Well, perhaps I will see you. I would like very much to talk more with you."

"No problem. You come, too."

"OK."

Cassio went after Bianca.

Othello came out of hiding and asked, "How shall I murder him, Iago?"

"Did you see how he laughed at his vice?" Iago asked.

"I did!"

"And did you see the handkerchief?"

Othello knew that the handkerchief was his, but he sadly asked, "Was that mine?"

"I swear that it was your handkerchief," Iago replied. "And you can see how much he values your wife, that foolish woman! Your wife gave him that handkerchief, and he gave it to his whore."

"I would like to take nine years to torture and kill him!" Othello said, adding sarcastically, "My wife is a fine woman, a fair woman, a sweet woman!"

"No, you must not think about that," Iago said.

"Let her rot!" Othello said. "Let her perish. Let her be damned tonight. She shall no longer live. My heart has turned to stone."

He hit himself in the chest and said, "When I hit my heart, my hand hurts. The world does not have a sweeter woman than my wife. She could lie beside an emperor and give him orders."

"This is not the best way for you to act."

"Hang her! I do but say what she is. She is so delicate with her needlework; she is an admirable musician! When she sings, she makes a savage bear become gentle. She is very witty and imaginative."

"She's all the worse for having so many fine qualities and yet being evil."

"Oh, a thousand thousand times, and also she is nobly born and has a gentle and yielding disposition."

"Yes, too yielding."

"That is certain, but it is such a pity, Iago! Such a pity!"

"If you are so foolish as to accept her unfaithfulness to you, then let her run wild and cuckold you. If that does not bother you, it will not bother anyone else."

"I will chop her into small pieces of meat!" Othello said. "She has cuckolded me!"

"It was foul of her."

"With my own officer!"

"That's fouler."

"Get me some poison, Iago, this very night. I will not talk to her, lest her body and beauty change my mind. Get it tonight, Iago."

"Don't kill her with poison. Strangle her in her bed — the bed she has contaminated."

"Good, good," Othello said. "The poetic justice of it pleases me very well."

"And as for Cassio, let me undertake his murder. You shall hear more by midnight."

"Excellent."

A trumpet sounded, and Othello said, "What is the purpose of that trumpet sounding?"

"It is surely a message from Venice. I see Lodovico coming toward us. The Duke of Venice must have sent him here. Look, your wife is with him."

Lodovico, Desdemona, and some attendants walked up to Othello and Iago.

"God bless you, worthy general!" Lodovico said.

"I thank you with all my heart, sir," Othello replied.

"The Duke and senators of Venice greet you and have sent you this letter."

He handed the letter to Othello.

"I kiss the instrument of their pleasures," Othello said courteously. He kissed the letter and then opened it and began to read it.

"What news have you brought, kinsman Lodovico?" Desdemona asked.

She came from a noble and well-known family and was related to many important men in Venice.

Iago said to Lodovico, "I am very glad to see you, signior. Welcome to Cyprus."

"I thank you. How is Lieutenant Cassio?"

"He lives, sir," Iago replied quietly, implying that something was wrong.

"Kinsman, there has fallen between Cassio and my husband an unnatural breach, but you shall make all well between them," Desdemona said.

"Are you sure of that?" Othello asked.

"My lord?" Desdemona replied. "What do you mean?"

Othello read part of the letter out loud, "*Do not fail to do this —*"

"Othello will not answer you right now," Lodovico said. "He is busy reading the letter. What is this about a breach between Cassio and Othello?"

"It is very unfortunate," Desdemona said. "I would do much to reconcile them because I respect Cassio's good qualities so much."

Overhearing her, Othello said, "Damn, damn, and damn!"

"My lord?" Desdemona asked. "What's wrong?"

"Haven't you any intelligence at all?" Othello said.

"What — are you angry?" Desdemona asked.

"Maybe the letter has angered him," Lodovico said. "I understand that his orders are to return to Venice and to leave Cassio here as governor in charge of Cyprus."

"I am glad that those are the orders," Desdemona said.

"Indeed!" Othello said.

"My lord?" Desdemona asked. "What's wrong?"

"I am happy to see that you have completely lost your mind," Othello said, thinking that she was mocking him by praising Cassio and being glad of Cassio's promotion.

"Why, darling Othello —" Desdemona began.

Othello struck her and said, "Devil!"

Shocked, and crying, Desdemona said, "I have not deserved this."

Also shocked, Lodovico said to Othello, "My lord, this would not be believed in Venice even if I swore that I saw it with my own eyes. Make this up to Desdemona. Apologize. She is crying."

"She is a devil!" Othello said. "If this woman's tears could impregnate the Earth, each tear she lets fall would produce a crocodile, which lures its prey near with its crocodile's tears."

He shouted at Desdemona, "Get out of my sight!"

"I will not stay here and offend you with my sight," Desdemona said and obediently left.

"Truly, she is an obedient lady," Lodovico said. "That is what a wife should be. I beg your lordship, please call her back and apologize to her."

"Mistress!" Othello called.

"My lord?" Desdemona asked. "What do you want?"

"What do you want to do with and to her, sir?" Othello asked Lodovico.

"Who, I, my lord?" Lodovico asked.

"Yes, you said that you wanted me to ask her to turn back. Sir, she can turn, and turn, and yet go on, and turn again."

Yes, Othello thought. *She can turn to one sexual position and then another sexual position and then yet another sexual position. And she can service one brothel customer and then another brothel customer and then yet another brothel customer.*

Othello added, "And she can weep, sir, she can weep."

Yes, Othello thought. *She can weep crocodile tears.*

Othello added, "And she's obedient, as you say, obedient, very obedient."

Yes, Othello thought. *She obeys Cassio's orders in bed.*

Othello ordered Desdemona, "Keep crying."

"About this letter, sir —" Othello began saying to Lodovico.

He said to Desdemona, "You fake sadness so well!"

He said to Lodovico, "I am commanded to return to Venice."

He said to Desdemona, "Get away from me. I will send for you soon."

He said to Lodovico, "Sir, I will obey my orders; I will return to Venice."

He shouted at Desdemona, "Leave me! Now!"

Desdemona left.

He said to Lodovico, "Cassio shall take over my place as governor. And, sir, I ask you to dine with me tonight. You are welcome, sir, to Cyprus."

Overcome by anger at the thought of Cassio and Desdemona in bed together, Othello shouted the names of two animals known for their horniness: "Goats and monkeys!"

He departed.

Shocked by what he had witnessed, Lodovico said to Iago, "Is this the noble Moor whom our entire senate regards with such esteem? Is this the man with such a reputation for self-control? Is this the man whose excellence and virtue cannot be harmed by either a cannon shot of fortune or an arrow of fate? Othello is supposed to be able to maintain his self-control and composure no matter what enemy forces he faces."

Iago replied, "He is much changed."

"Is his mind sound? Has he become insane?" Lodovico asked.

"He is what he is. As an officer serving under him, I ought not to state my opinion about his state of mind, but if he is not insane, I wish to God that he were because that would excuse his actions!"

"He actually struck his wife!"

"That was an evil action, but I wish that I knew that that was the most evil thing he would do!"

"Is this the way that he usually acts?" Lodovico asked Iago. "Or is he so upset by the letter that he is acting abnormally?"

"I am sorry, but as his officer I ought not to speak about what I have seen and known him to do. You should watch him — his own actions will reveal his character to you and so I need not reveal his character by talking about it. Watch him, and see how he acts."

"I am sorry that I was mistaken about his character," Lodovico said.

In a room in the castle, Othello was questioning Emilia, Desdemona's attendant and Iago's wife.

"You have seen nothing suspicious?"

"I have never seen or heard anything suspicious," Emilia replied, "and I have never suspected Desdemona of doing anything wrong."

"You have seen Cassio and her together."

"Yes, but I have never seen them do anything wrong, and I have heard every syllable that they have spoken to each other."

"Did they ever whisper?"

"Never, my lord."

"And they never sent you away?"

"Never."

"Not even to fetch her fan, her gloves, her mask, or something else?"

"Never, my lord."

"That's strange."

"I would bet my immortal soul that she is faithful to you. If you think otherwise, you are wrong and you need to change your thinking. Remove any thought that Desdemona has done you wrong; such thoughts abuse your heart. If any wretch has put such a thought in your head, let Heaven repay that deed with the serpent's curse! Remember Genesis 3:14-15: '*And the Lord God said unto the serpent, Because thou hast done this, thou art cursed above all cattle, and above every beast of the field; upon thy belly shalt thou go, and dust shalt thou eat all the days of thy life: And I will put enmity between thee and the woman, and between thy seed and her seed; it shall bruise thy head, and thou shalt bruise his heel.*' If Desdemona is not honest, chaste, and true to you, then no man is happy — the purest of their wives is as foul as slander."

"Tell Desdemona to come here," Othello said. "Go now."

Emilia left the room.

Othello said to himself, "She says that Desdemona is faithful to me, but it would have to be a stupid and foolish brothel-keeper who would not lie as well as Emilia. Emilia is a subtle whore who acts like a lock and key and keeps villainous secrets, and yet she kneels and prays — I have seen her do it."

Desdemona and Emilia both entered the room.

"My lord, what is your will?" Desdemona asked.

"Please, chick, come here," Othello said.

Desdemona walked to Othello and asked, "What do you want?"

"Let me see your eyes; look at my face," Othello angrily said.

Wary, Desdemona asked, "What horrible notion is this?"

Othello said to Emilia, "Do your job, mistress. Leave us procreants — we who procreate — alone and shut the door. Cough, or cry 'ahem,' if anybody comes. That is your job, so do it."

Emilia knew that she had been insulted. The words that Othello had used implied that she was the keeper of a brothel and that her job was to help people have illicit and immoral sex. But she was afraid, and she left.

Desdemona, who knew much less of the evils of the world than Emilia, understood the tone of voice that Othello had used. She knelt before Othello and said, "What do you mean? I understand from your tone of voice that you are angry, but I do not understand your words."

"Why, what are you?" Othello asked her.

"Your wife, my lord; your true, faithful, and loyal wife."

"Come, swear it, and damn yourself," Othello said. "You are beautiful, and you look like you belong in Heaven. I do not want the devils of Hell to be afraid to seize you after you die, so therefore swear to me that you are faithful to me, and be double-damned."

He thought, *Be damned once for adultery and once for perjury.*

"Heaven knows that I am faithful to you."

"Heaven knows that you are as false as Hell."

"To whom am I false, my lord? With whom am I false? How am I false?"

"Desdemona, stay away from me!" Othello said, crying.

"This is a horrible day," Desdemona said. "Why are you crying? Am I the reason for these tears, my lord? If you suspect that my father is the cause of your being recalled to Venice, do not blame me. If you have lost his good will, I also have lost his good will."

"Had it pleased Heaven to test me by afflicting me, by raining all kinds of sores and shames on my bare head, by steeping me in poverty up to my lips, by imprisoning me and chaining up all my hopes, I still would have found in some place of my soul a drop of patience. Unfortunately, Heaven has made me a fixed figure for everyone to scorn and to point at like the numbers on a clock. It is as if my disgrace were written on the face of a clock in the marketplace. Still, I could bear that, too, well — very well. But in the place where I have given my heart, where either I must live, or have no life, where is the fountain from which my current runs, or else dries up — I am referring to you, my wife — I have been thrown out from that place, I have been discarded from there! It is now a cistern where foul toads copulate and breed. Change your complexion, like the young and rose-lipped cherub known as Patience when she looks at the place where I have given my heart. That's right — now you look as grim as Hell!"

"I hope my noble lord believes that I am honest and faithful to him and morally pure."

"Yes, I do believe that you are chaste," Othello said sarcastically. "As chaste as summer flies are in the slaughterhouses, flies that become pregnant again as soon as their eggs are laid. You weed, you are so lovely and so beautiful and you smell so sweet that my senses ache when they behold you — I wish that you had never been born!"

"What sin have I committed without being aware of it?" Desdemona asked.

Othello looked at Desdemona's face and said, "Was this beautiful paper, this excellent book, made to write the word 'whore' upon? What sin have you committed!"

He thought, *You know Exodus 20:14; it is one of the Ten Commandments: "Thou shalt not commit adultery."*

He said, "You are a common whore! I should make forges of my cheeks; they would burn with embarrassment if I were to mention your evil deeds out loud. What sin have you committed! Heaven stops its nose at it so it will not smell your sin and the Moon — a symbol of chastity — closes its eyes so it will not see your sin. Even the bawdy wind that kisses all it meets is hiding in a hollow cave under the ground so it will not hear about your sin. What sin have you committed! You are an impudent whore!"

"By Heaven, you do me wrong," Desdemona said.

"Are you not a whore?"

"No, I am not. I swear it as I am a Christian," Desdemona said. "If to preserve this vessel — my body — for my lord from any foul unlawful touch means that I am not a whore, then I am not a whore."

"What? You say that you are not a whore?"

"I am not a whore. If I am, then I give up my eternal salvation eternally."

"Is it possible that you can say such a thing?"

"Heaven forgive us!"

"I beg your pardon, then," Othello said sarcastically. "I mistook you for that cunning whore of Venice who married Othello."

Othello raised his voice and called Emilia: "You, mistress, who have the office opposite to that of Saint Peter, and keep the gate of Hell while he keeps the gate of Heaven, come here."

Emilia entered the room.

Othello threw a few coins at her and said, "We have finished; here's money for your pains. Please, keep the door and keep the secrets of Desdemona and me."

He left the room.

Emilia knew that she and Desdemona had been insulted. Othello was treating Desdemona like a whore and Emilia like the keeper of a brothel. He was acting as if he had been one of a whore's — Desdemona's — customers and was tipping Emilia for her services as a procurer and to have her not gossip about his use of a prostitute's services.

Emilia said, "What is going on in your husband's brain? How are you, madam? How are you, my good lady?"

"I am in shock. It is as if I am half-asleep."

"Good madam, what's the matter with my lord?"

"With whom?"

"Why, with my lord, madam."

"Who is your lord?"

"The same person who is your lord, your husband, sweet lady."

"I have no lord, no husband," Desdemona replied. "Do not talk to me, Emilia. I cannot cry, and tears would accompany the only answers that I can give you. Please, lay my wedding sheets on my bed tonight. Remember that. Also, call your husband here so I can talk to him."

"Things have certainly changed around here!" Emilia said.

She left to get her husband, Iago.

Desdemona said sadly but sarcastically and bitterly, "It is fitting that I should be treated this way, very fitting. What have I done that he should make even the smallest criticism about my greatest fault?"

Emilia and Iago entered the room.

Iago looked at Desdemona, whom he was hoping to manipulate her husband into murdering, and asked, "What do you want, madam? How are you?"

"I do not know how I am," Desdemona replied. "Those who teach young babes do so gently and give them easy tasks to do. My husband might have criticized me gently because, indeed, like a child I am unaccustomed to being scolded."

"What's the matter, lady?" Iago asked.

"It's a shame, Iago, but my lord treated her as if she were a whore. He has called her spiteful and scornful names that good people cannot bear."

"Am I deserving of the names he called me, Iago?" Desdemona asked.

"What names, fair lady?"

"Such names as your wife says my lord did say I was."

"He called her a whore," Emilia said. "Not even a drunk beggar would have called his slut such names as Othello called Desdemona."

"Why did he do that?" Iago asked.

"I do not know why," Desdemona said. "I am sure that I did not deserve to be called such names."

"Do not cry, Desdemona, do not cry," Iago said. "This is a sorrowful day!"

"Has Desdemona given up so many noble marriages that she could have made, has she given up her father and her country and her friends, just to end up being called a whore?" Emilia said. "Doesn't this make you want to cry?"

"It is my wretched fate," Desdemona said.

"Curse him for this," Iago said. "Why is he acting this way?"

"I don't know," Desdemona said. "Only Heaven knows."

"I can guess the cause," Emilia said. "I will be hanged if some eternal villain, if some busy and insinuating rogue, if some lying, cheating slave, to get some job, has not devised some slander. I will be hanged if this is not true."

Iago said, "No man can be that evil. That is impossible," but he thought, *That is a good part of the truth — I did it in part so that I could be lieutenant, and now I am lieutenant.*

"If any such man exists, may Heaven pardon him!" Desdemona said.

"May a halter around his neck pardon him!" Emilia said. "And may Hell gnaw his bones! Why should Othello call Desdemona a whore? How is it even possible for her to have an affair? Who keeps her company that she could have an affair with? In what place could an affair take place? At what time could an affair take place? How could an affair happen? What is the evidence for an affair? Some very villainous knave, some base and notorious knave, some scurvy fellow has abused the Moor. I wish that Heaven would reveal such villains for what they are and put in every honest hand a whip to lash the rascals naked through the world from the East to the West!"

Iago did not like hearing his wife say this. He said, "Speak more quietly. We are indoors."

"To Hell with such men!" Emilia said. "Such a man spoke with you and turned your brain inside out and made you suspect that I had an affair with the Moor."

Iago replied, "You are a fool. Shut up."

Desdemona said, "Good Iago, what can I do to win my lord again? Good friend, go to him and talk to him. By this light of Heaven, the Sun, I swear that I do not know how I lost him. Here I kneel and swear that if ever my will trespassed against his love, either in thought or in actual deed, then may I never be happy. I swear that if my eyes, my ears, or any other sense ever delight in any man except my husband, then may I never be happy. I swear that if I never dearly loved my husband or do not dearly love my husband now or do not continue to dearly love my husband — even if he were to shake me off and divorce me and make me a beggar — then may I never be happy. Unkindness may do much, and his unkindness may take away my life, but it can never take away my love for him. I can hardly say the word 'whore' — to say the word now abhors me. I would not do the act that would make me a whore for all the world's mass of vain finery."

"Please, control yourself," Iago said. "This is a temporary mood of Othello's. He is bothered by affairs of state and so he quarrels with you."

"I hope that is the reason and there is nothing else —" Desdemona began.

Iago interrupted, "That is the reason. I promise you that."

Trumpets sounded.

Iago said, "The trumpets are sounding to announce that the evening meal is ready. Your guests — the messengers from Venice — are ready to dine. Go in to the meal, and do not cry. Don't worry — all shall be well."

Desdemona and Emilia went in to the meal, while Iago went outside, where he found an angry Roderigo waiting for him.

"How are you, Roderigo?"

"You have not been treating me fairly!"

"What have I done to make you think that?"

"Every day you put me off with some excuse, Iago. It seems to me now that you keep me from taking advantage of any and all opportunities that would further me even a little in my pursuit of Desdemona. I have not even met Desdemona. I will no longer endure it, and I am not about to let you get away with having treated me this badly."

"Listen to me, Roderigo —"

"I have listened to you too much already because your words and your actions do not match."

"You accuse me most unjustly."

"My accusation is nothing but true," Roderigo said. "I have wasted my capital. The jewels you have received from me to give to Desdemona would have half corrupted a Catholic nun. You have told me that Desdemona has received my gifts and in return has given to you to deliver to me words of hope and expectation that she and I will meet on intimate terms, but that never happens."

"Well, go on. Continue," Iago said.

"Go on! Continue!" Roderigo said. "I cannot go on and continue. My money is almost gone. I am in a scurvy situation, and I think that you have cheated me."

"Go on."

"I tell you that I cannot go on in this way. I intend to introduce myself to Desdemona and tell her that if she returns my jewels to me, I will stop pursuing her and repent my immoral solicitation of a married woman. If she will not return my jewels to me, assure yourself that I will seek satisfaction from you."

Iago thought, *If he talks to Desdemona, he will discover that I have delivered to her no jewels. Instead, I put them in my pocket.*

"Have you said all you have to say?"

"Yes, and I have said nothing but what I intend to do."

"Why, I see that you have spunk, and I now have a better opinion of you than I ever had before," Iago said. "Shake my hand, Roderigo. You have greatly criticized me, but I say that I have always been honest in trying to help you achieve your goal of sleeping with Desdemona."

"It does not look like it."

"I grant that you have not yet enjoyed Desdemona's body, and so your suspicion of me is founded on intelligent and good judgment. But, Roderigo, if you have some qualities in you that I indeed have greater reason to believe now than ever before — I refer to purpose, courage, and valor — this night you need to prove that you have those qualities. Prove that this night, and if you are not enjoying Desdemona's body tomorrow night, then form treacherous plots against my life and kill me and take me from this world."

"What do you want me to do?" Roderigo said. "Is it something reasonable that can likely be accomplished? Is it feasible?"

"Sir, a letter from Venice has arrived with orders to replace Othello with Cassio as governor of Cyprus."

"Is that true? Why, then Othello and Desdemona will return to Venice."

"No," Iago lied. "Othello will go into Mauritania in Western Africa and take away with him the fair Desdemona, unless his stay here be lengthened by some event — definitely, if Cassio were to be removed, Othello and Desdemona would stay here in Cyprus."

"What do you mean by the removing of Cassio?"

"I mean that Cassio needs to be made incapable of taking Othello's place, as will be true if his brains are knocked out."

"And that is what you want me to do?"

"Yes, if you dare to do something that will profit you and give you something — Desdemona — that ought to be yours by right. Cassio is dining with a prostitute, and I will go and join them. Cassio does not yet know of his good and honorable fortune — his being made governor of Cyprus. If you will wait for him to leave, which I will make happen between midnight and one, you may kill him at your pleasure. I will be near to give you support, and with both of us attacking him, he shall die."

Roderigo looked shocked.

Iago said, "Come on. Don't just stand there. Come with me. I will give you such reasons why his death is necessary that you will feel obliged to kill him. It is now suppertime, and the time is passing quickly. Let's go."

"I need to hear further reasons why Cassio's death is necessary."

"And I will tell them to you," Iago replied.

They departed.

In a room in the castle were Othello, Lodovico, Desdemona, Emilia, and some attendants. The evening meal was over, and Othello was offering to walk Lodovico home.

Lodovico said to Othello, "Please, sir, trouble yourself no further about me."

"It is no trouble," Othello said. "A walk will do me good."

"Madam, good night," Lodovico said. "I humbly thank your ladyship."

"Your honor is most welcome," Desdemona replied courteously.

"Shall we walk, sir?" Othello asked Lodovico.

He then said, "Desdemona —"

"My lord?"

"Go to bed immediately. I will return soon. Send Emilia, your attendant, away, also. Make sure that you follow my orders."

"I will, my lord."

Othello, Lodovico, and some attendants exited.

Emilia had been far enough away that she had not heard what Othello had said. She said to Desdemona, "How is everything going now? Othello looks gentler and calmer than he did."

"He says that he will return quickly. He has ordered me to go to bed and to dismiss you. Apparently, he wants me to be alone when he returns."

"Dismiss me!" Emilia said, surprised. Normally, a lady's attendant would stay with her until the lady's husband was ready for bed.

"That is what he ordered," Desdemona said. "Therefore, good Emilia, give me my night clothes. We must not now displease him."

Uneasy, Emilia said, "I wish that you had never seen him!"

"I do not have that wish," Desdemona said. "I love him so much that even his stubbornness, his rebukes of me, his frowns — please, unpin my hair and dress — have grace and favor in them."

"I have laid on the bed those sheets you asked me to get."

"It doesn't matter. All's one. Good faith, how foolish are our minds! What thoughts they make us think! If I die before you, please use one of those sheets as my shroud."

"Come, that's no way to talk," Emilia said.

"My mother had a maid named Barbary, a form of Barbara. She was in love, and the man she loved proved to be unfaithful and forsook her, She used to sing a song named 'Willow.' The willow is a symbol of unrequited love; the weeping willow is a symbol of unhappiness. It was an old song, but it expressed her fortune, and she died singing it. That song tonight will not leave my mind. I find it difficult to keep from hanging my head to one side and singing that song like poor Barbary. Please, hurry up."

"Shall I go and fetch your nightgown?"

"No, finish unpinning me now," Desdemona said, adding, "This Lodovico is a proper man."

"A very handsome man."

"He speaks well."

"I know a lady in Venice who would have walked barefoot to Palestine for a kiss from him."

Had Desdemona not married Othello, she might have married a man much like Lodovico. Although he was a relative, if he were a distant enough relative, and unmarried, she might even have married Lodovico.

Desdemona began to sing:

"The poor soul sat sighing by a sycamore tree,

"Sing all a green willow:

"Her hand on her bosom, her head on her knee,

"Sing willow, willow, willow.

"The fresh streams ran by her, and repeated her moans;

"Sing willow, willow, willow.

"Her salt tears fell from her, and softened the stones."

She gave some clothing to Emilia and said, "Put these away."

Desdemona then sang again:

"Sing willow, willow, willow."

She said to Emilia, "Please, go now. Othello will soon return."

Desdemona then sang again:

"Sing, all — a green willow must be my garland.

"Let nobody blame him; his scorn I accept —"

She stopped and said, "No, that line is not next."

Hearing a noise, she said, "Listen! Who is knocking?"

Emilia replied, "It's the wind."

Desdemona then sang again:

"*I called my lover untrue, but what did he say then?*

"*Sing willow, willow, willow.*

"'*If I court more women, you'll sleep with more men!*'"

She said to Emilia, "Well, go now. My eyes itch. Is that a sign of weeping to come?"

"It is neither here nor there," Emilia said.

"I have heard it said that itchy eyes foretell weeping. Oh, these men, these men! Do you truly think — tell me, Emilia — that women really exist who abuse their husbands by making them cuckolds?"

"Some such women exist, no question about it."

"Would you do such a deed for all the world?"

"Why, wouldn't you?"

"No, by this Heavenly light, the Sun!"

"Neither would I in this Heavenly light from the Sun, but I might do it in the dark," Emilia said.

"Would you do such a deed for all the world?"

"The world is huge; it is very valuable. It is a great payment for performing a small vice."

"Truly, I don't think that you would ever be guilty of such a sin."

"Truly, I think that I would," Emilia said. "I would do the sin, and after I had the world, I would undo the damage resulting from the sin. Of course, I would not do such a thing for a ring, or for yards of fine linen, or for clothing such as gowns, petticoats, and caps, or for any petty amount of money or petty gift — but for the whole world? Why, who would not make her husband a cuckold if it would make him a monarch? I would risk being condemned to much time in Purgatory for committing such a sin. This sin can be forgiven; it need not result in being condemned to Hell."

"Curse me if I would do such a wrong even for the whole world."

"Why, the wrong is only a wrong in the world. Once you have the world as the price for your labor, it is a wrong in your own world, and you might quickly make it right."

"I do not think that any such woman exists who would commit such a sin."

"Yes, a dozen, and as many in addition as would fill the world they played for. But I think it is their husbands' faults if wives fall into this kind of sin. Husbands sometimes slack in their duties — instead of sleeping with us, they pour their treasured semen into the laps of other women. Or else the husbands break out in peevish jealousies and restrict our freedom. Or they strike us. Or they reduce our monetary allowance out of spite. Why, we have spirits that can feel resentment, and though we have some grace and can forgive them, yet sometimes we want and get revenge. Let husbands know that their wives have senses and feelings just like theirs: They see and smell and have an appetite both for sweet and sour, just like husbands have. What is it that husbands get when they exchange us — their legitimate wives — for others? Is it sexual pleasure? I think it is. Does affection breed it? I think it does. Is it frailty that thus errs? Yes. Don't we wives have affections, desires for sexual pleasure, and frailty, as men have? Then let them treat us well, or else let them know that the sins we do, their own sins teach us to do."

Desdemona said, "Good night, good night. May Heaven help me learn from such examples to avoid doing evil!"

Emilia exited, leaving Desdemona alone in the bedchamber.

CHAPTER 5

— 5.1 —

Iago and Roderigo spoke together on a dark street near where Cassio was visiting Bianca.

Iago said, "Here, stand behind this projecting wall. Cassio will arrive quickly. Take out your rapier, and thrust it deep in him. Quick, quick; don't be afraid. I will be at your elbow. This action will make us, or it will mar us and ruin us; think about that, and be resolute."

"Be close at hand," Roderigo said. "I may need help."

"Here I am, by your side," Iago said. "Be bold, and take your stand."

Iago withdrew a short distance away.

I have no great desire to do this deed of murder, Roderigo thought. *And yet Iago has given me reasons for committing murder. Oh, well. It is only the death of a single man. I will draw my sword — Cassio will die tonight.*

Iago thought, *I have rubbed this pimple — this youngster, this Roderigo — until it is raw, and now he grows angry at me. Now, whether Roderigo kills Cassio, or Cassio kills him, or each kills the other, I come out ahead. If Roderigo stays alive, he will demand that I make a large restitution to him — he will demand that I restore to him all the gold and jewels that I defrauded him, saying that they were gifts for Desdemona when actually I put them in my own pocket. That must not happen. If Cassio should stay alive, he has a constant beauty of character in his life that makes me ugly by comparison and, in addition, the Moor may eventually talk to him and learn that I have been lying about Desdemona. Because of that, I stand in much danger, and so Cassio must die. Listen! I hear him coming!*

Cassio arrived.

Roderigo thought, *I know his gait — he is Cassio.*

He then said to Cassio, "Villain, now you must die!"

He thrust his sword at Cassio, who said, "That sword thrust would have been my death, but I am a soldier and I am wearing a privy coat — a coat of mail underneath my regular clothing — for protection. Now let us see whether your coat is as good as mine."

Cassio thrust his sword into Roderigo's body, and Roderigo cried, "I am going to die!"

In the dark, Iago came up behind Cassio. Knowing that Cassio was wearing a protective coat of mail, Iago wounded him in the leg with his sword and then fled.

Cassio shouted, "I am maimed forever! Murder! Murder!"

He fell.

Othello, who was walking to his home after having walked Lodovico home, heard the noise and thought, *It is the voice of Cassio; Iago has kept his word and murdered him.*

Roderigo shouted, "Damn me!"

Othello thought, *Cassio should be damned.*

Cassio shouted, "Help! Bring some light here! I need a doctor!"

Othello thought, *Yes, it is the voice of Cassio. Brave Iago, you are honest and just. You have a noble sense of the wrong done to me, your friend! You teach me how to act now.*

He thought about Desdemona, *Hussy, your dear lies dead, and your cursed end hurries to you. Whore, I am coming to see you. Your charming eyes no longer influence my heart. You have spotted our bed with lust, and now I shall spot it with your whorish blood.*

Othello departed.

Lodovico had decided to take a walk with his friend Gratiano and seek Cassio.

Cassio shouted, "Help! Are there no watchmen? No passersby to help me? Murder! Murder!"

"Something bad has happened," Gratiano said. "Someone badly needs assistance."

Cassio shouted, "Help!"

Lodovico said, "Listen!"

Roderigo shouted, "Damn!"

"Two or three men are groaning," Lodovico said. "It is a dark night. Let's be careful. These men may be acting as if they are hurt so that they can rob us when we come to their assistance. Let's get more people and then go to them."

Lodovico was understandably cautious because he was in a country that was not his own.

"Is nobody coming to help me?" Roderigo shouted. "Then I shall bleed to death."

Lodovico said again, "Listen!"

Iago now returned.

Gratiano said, "Here comes someone wearing a nightshirt and carrying a lamp and a sword."

"Who's there?" Iago said. "Who is shouting, 'Murder!'?"

"We do not know," Lodovico said.

"Did you hear anyone shout?" Iago asked.

"Here, here!" Cassio shouted, "For Heaven's sake, help me!"

Iago asked, "What's the matter?"

Gratiano said, "I recognize this man. This is Othello's ancient."

"You are right," Lodovico said. "He is Iago, a very valiant fellow."

"Who are you here who is shouting so grievously?" Iago asked.

Cassio replied, "Is that you, Iago? I am wounded, injured by villains. Give me some help."

"Lieutenant, what villains have done this?" Iago asked.

"I think that one of them is still near here and cannot flee."

"They are treacherous villains!" Iago said.

Seeing Lodovico and Gratiano, he said, "Who are you there? Come here, and give us some help."

Roderigo shouted, "Help me! I am over here!"

"That is one of the men who attacked me," Cassio said.

Iago went over to Roderigo and said, "You murderous slave! You villain!"

Then he stabbed Roderigo, who weakly said, "Damn you, Iago! You inhuman dog!"

Roderigo fainted and appeared to be dead.

"Killing men in the dark!" Iago shouted. "Where are these bloody thieves? How quiet the town is tonight! Murder! Murder!"

Seeing Lodovico and Gratiano, Iago asked, "Who are you! Are you good men or bad men?"

"Judge us by our actions, then praise us," Lodovico said.

Iago asked, "Are you Signior Lodovico?"

"Yes."

"I beg your pardon. Here is Cassio. He has been hurt by villains."

"Cassio!" Gratiano said.

"How are you, brother?" Iago asked Cassio.

"My leg has been cut in two."

"Heaven forbid!" Iago exclaimed. "Hold the lamp so I have light, gentlemen. I will bandage Cassio's wound with my shirt."

The attack had occurred outside Bianca's home. She had heard the noise and now came running.

She asked, "What is the matter? Who is he who cried out?"

"Who is he who cried out?" Iago repeated, sarcastically, implying that Bianca knew who had cried out.

Bianca saw the wounded Cassio and exclaimed, "Oh, my dear Cassio! My sweet Cassio! Cassio, Cassio, Cassio!"

"You are a notable whore!" Iago said to her.

He then asked, "Cassio, do you know which men wounded you?"

"No."

Gratiano said to Cassio, "I am sorry to see that you are wounded. I was on my way to find you."

"Someone, lend me a garter so I can bind Cassio's bandage," Iago said. "Good. Now we need a sedan chair — an enclosed chair attached to two poles so that servants can carry it — so that we can easily carry Cassio to a doctor."

"Cassio has fainted from loss of blood," Bianca cried.

Iago said, "Gentlemen, I do suspect this trash — this woman — to be a party in this attack against Cassio."

He said to Cassio, "Be patient. We will take care of you."

He then walked over to where Roderigo was lying and said, "Bring a lamp here. Do we know this man? It is my friend and my dear countryman Roderigo! Is it? No — yes, it is, definitely. Oh, Heaven! It is Roderigo."

"Roderigo of Venice?" Gratiano asked.

"Yes, it is he, sir," Iago asked. "Did you know him?"

"Know him? Yes."

"Is that you, Signior Gratiano?" Iago said. "Please pardon me. This bloody attack must excuse my bad manners — I did not mean to neglect you."

"I am glad to see you," Gratiano said.

"How are you doing, Cassio?" Iago asked. "We need a sedan chair! A chair!"

Gratiano looked at Roderigo and said, "Roderigo!"

"Yes, it is he," Iago said.

Some people arrived, carrying a sedan chair, and Iago said, "Well done. Some good men carry Cassio carefully from here; I'll get the general's surgeon."

He said to Bianca, "As for you, mistress, keep out of the way."

He said to Cassio, "The man who lies here dead was my dear friend. His name was Roderigo. What was the problem between you two?"

"There was none," Cassio said. "I don't even know the man."

Iago said to Bianca, "You look pale. That is suspicious."

He then said, "Carry Cassio away."

Cassio was carried away in the sedan chair. Some men also carried away Roderigo.

Iago said to Lodovico and Gratiano, "Stay here a moment, gentlemen."

He said to Bianca, "Do you look pale, mistress?"

He said to Lodovico and Gratiano, "Do you see the terror in her eyes?"

He said to Bianca, "Go ahead and stare. We shall learn more soon."

He said to Lodovico and Gratiano, "Look at her closely. See how guilty she looks! Guilt will reveal itself even when tongues stay silent."

Emilia walked up to Iago and the others and asked, "What is going on? What's the matter, husband?"

Iago replied, "Cassio has here been attacked in the dark by Roderigo and some fellows who have escaped. Cassio is close to dying, and Roderigo is dead."

"This is a pity, good gentlemen!" Emilia said. "It is a shame that this happened to good Cassio!"

"This is the fruit of whoring," Iago said. "Please, Emilia, go to Cassio and ask him where he dined this night."

He looked at Bianca and asked, "Are you shaking with fear because of what I asked my wife to do?"

"Cassio dined at my house tonight, but I am not shivering in this cool night air because of that."

"Oh, so he did dine with you," Iago said. "I command you to come with me."

"Damn you, whore," Emilia said.

"I am no whore," Bianca said. "I live as respectable a life as you who are verbally abusing me."

"As respectable a life as I!" Emilia said. "Not likely!"

Iago said, "Kind gentlemen, let's go and make sure that poor Cassio's wounds are bandaged."

He said to Bianca, "Come, mistress, you must tell us another tale."

He said to his wife, "Emilia, run to the citadel and tell the Moor and Desdemona what has happened."

He said to Lodovico and Gratiano, "Please lead the way."

He thought, *This is the night that will either make me or entirely ruin me.*

Desdemona was asleep in her bedchamber in the castle. A candle was burning near her.

Othello entered the room and thought this:

It is the cause; it is the cause, my soul. Let me not name it to you, you chaste stars! It is the cause.

I must keep in mind the cause. Desdemona has committed adultery, and that is the cause — the reason — why I must punish her.

I will not shed her blood, and I will not scar that whiter skin of hers than snow — that skin as smooth as alabaster stone used in making tombs. Yet she must die, else she will betray more men.

I will put out the candle's light, and then I will put out the light that is her life. If I quench you, you flaming candle, I can easily again restore your light, if I repent my action. But if I put out the light that is Desdemona's life — that pattern so skillfully wrought by nature excelling itself — I do not know where to find the heat that Prometheus used when he created human beings and so I cannot make you live again.

When I have plucked a rose, I cannot give it vital growth again. It must wither and it will wither. So will it be if I pluck your life, Desdemona.

I'll smell the rose on the bush.

He leaned down and kissed Desdemona.

He thought, *Your breath is fragrant. It almost persuades Justice to break her sword of punishment! One more kiss, one more. Be like this when you are dead, and I will kill you and love you afterward.*

He kissed her.

One more, and this is the last kiss, he thought.

He kissed her a third time.

So sweet was never so fatal. I must weep, but I weep cruel tears. This sorrow is Heavenly — it strikes where it does love. I remember Proverbs 3:12: "For whom the LORD loveth he correcteth." She is waking up.

Desdemona asked, "Who's there? Othello?"

"Yes, Desdemona."

"Will you come to bed, my lord?"

"Have you prayed tonight, Desdemona?"

"Yes, my lord."

"If you can think of any sin that you have not confessed and asked to be forgiven for, pray about it immediately. You must be reconciled with God and forgiven by Him."

"That sounds ominous. My lord, what do you mean by that?"

"Do it now, and be brief; I will walk nearby to give you some privacy. I would not kill your unprepared spirit. You must be ready to enter Heaven. I would not kill your soul — Heaven forbid that!"

"Are you talking about killing me?"

"Yes, I am."

"Then I pray that Heaven have mercy on me!"

"Amen, with all my heart!" Othello said.

"If you can say that, I hope that you will have mercy on me and not kill me."

"What you hope — that will not happen."

"I fear you. You are deadly when your eyes roll like they are doing now. But I do not know why I should be afraid that you will kill me. I have done nothing wrong and I am guilty of nothing, and yet I am afraid that you will kill me."

"Think about your sin."

"My sin is the love I have for you," Desdemona said.

She added, "It is a sin to love a mortal man more than God."

"True, and that is the reason you will die," Othello said, thinking that Desdemona loved Cassio.

"Death is most unnatural when one kills because of love," Desdemona said. "Why are you gnawing your lower lip? Some bloody passion shakes your very frame: These are deadly portents; but yet I hope, I hope, that they do not pertain to me."

"Be quiet, and be still!"

"I will obey you," Desdemona said. "What's the matter?"

"That handkerchief that I so valued and gave to you, you gave to Cassio."

"No, by my life and soul that is not true! Send for the man, and ask him."

"Sweet soul, take heed and be careful not to commit the sin of perjury. You are on your deathbed."

"I may eventually die in this bed, but not yet, I hope."

"You will die very soon on this bed. Therefore, confess freely your sins. Denying anything of which you are accused will not remove or strangle the strong suspicions that make me groan. You will die."

"Then, Lord God, have mercy on me!"

"To that I say, 'Amen.'"

"And, Lord my husband, you have mercy on me, too! I have never done anything to offend you in my life. I have never had anything to do with Cassio except what Heaven would approve of. I have never given him any love-token, including your handkerchief."

"By Heaven, I saw my handkerchief in his hand," Othello said. "Woman, you have committed the sin of perjury. You have turned my heart to stone. Your refusal to confess your sins forces me to call what I intend to do a murder, which I thought would instead be a sacrificial gesture. I saw the handkerchief."

"Then he found it. I never gave it to him. Send for him — he will tell you the truth."

"He has confessed the truth."

"What, my lord?"

"He has confessed that he has used you."

"How? Immorally?"

"Yes. He has confessed that you and he have committed adultery."

"Call him here. He will not say that."

"No, he won't. His mouth is closed and will never again open. Honest Iago has seen to that."

"I am afraid! Is Cassio dead?"

"Had all his hairs been lives, my great desire for revenge would have ended each life."

"He has been betrayed, and I will die."

She cried.

"Stop, whore! Will you cry for Cassio in front of me?"

"Banish me, my lord. Send me away, but do not kill me!"

"Don't you move, whore!"

"Kill me tomorrow — let me live tonight!"

Othello grabbed her and said, "Don't you struggle —"

"Let me live another half an hour!"

"Now that I have started, I must go on."

"Wait until I say one prayer!"

"It is too late."

Othello strangled Desdemona, his wife.

Emilia, outside the bedchamber door, called, "My lord! My lord!"

Othello listened to hear whether Desdemona was breathing; he said, "What noise is this? Not dead? Not yet quite dead? I who am cruel am also merciful. I would not have you linger in pain."

He put his hands around her neck again and squeezed.

Emilia called, "My lord! My lord!"

"Who's there?" Othello called.

"My good lord, I need to talk to you!"

"It is Emilia," Othello said.

He called, "Wait a moment!"

He thought, *Desdemona is dead. Likely, Emilia has come to inform me about Cassio's death. The attack and its aftermath created a lot of noise. Desdemona is no longer moving — she is as still as the grave. Shall I let Emilia come in? Is that what I should do? Is Desdemona moving? No. What is the best thing for me to do? If Emilia comes in, she'll want to speak to my wife. My wife! My wife! What wife? I have no wife. This is unbearable! This is a heavy hour! I think a huge eclipse of Sun and Moon should occur now, and I think that the frightened globe should tear itself apart in an earthquake. Now the world should end.*

Emilia called, "Please, I need to talk to you, my good Lord!"

"I had forgotten about you," Othello said. "Come in, Emilia. Wait a moment. Let me first draw the curtains around the bed. Now I will unlock the door."

He unlocked the door and let Emilia in and said, "What's the matter with you now?"

"My good Lord, murders have been committed!"

"When? Just now?

"Just now, my Lord."

"The Moon has caused this. She errs in her orbit and comes closer to the Earth than usual, and she is making men lunatics."

"My Lord, Cassio has killed a young Venetian named Roderigo."

"Roderigo has been killed!" Othello said. "And Cassio has been killed!"

"No, Cassio has not been killed."

"Cassio has not been killed!" Othello said.

He thought, *Murder is out of tune, and the sounds of sweet revenge grow harsh. The wrong man has been killed.*

Desdemona revived and said, "I have been unfairly murdered!"

"What cry is that?" Emilia asked.

"That! What?" Othello said.

"That was my lady's voice," Emilia said.

Emilia cried, "Help! Help! Help!" and ran to the bed.

She held Desdemona in her arms and said, "Oh, lady, speak again! Sweet Desdemona! Oh, sweet mistress, speak!"

"I die a guiltless death," Desdemona said. "I have done nothing wrong."

"Who has done this deed?" Emilia asked.

Wanting to protect her husband, Desdemona said, "Nobody; I have done it myself. Farewell. Give my love to my kind lord. Oh, farewell!"

Desdemona died.

Othello said, "How can she have been murdered? Who could have murdered her?"

"Who knows?" Emilia replied.

"You heard her say herself that it was not I."

"She said so. My duty is to report the truth."

"Like the liar she is, she has gone to burning Hell. I am the person who killed her."

"Then the more angel she, and you the blacker devil! With her final words, she forgave you and tried to make you appear innocent of her murder."

"She turned to sin, and she was a whore," Othello said.

"You are telling lies about her, and you are a devil."

"She was false as water. She was as changeable as the tides. Water is unstable — it often changes; it can be liquid water, ice, snow, and water vapor. She was beautiful on the outside, but that appearance was deceptive."

"You are as rash as fire when you say that she was false. She was as true as Heaven! She was not deceitful or sinful."

"Cassio lay on top of her," Othello said. "Ask your husband whether that is true. I would be damned to Hell for eternity if I murdered Desdemona without just cause. Your husband knows that she was false to me."

"My husband?"

"Your husband."

"He knew that Desdemona committed adultery and broke the marriage vows she made in church?"

"Yes, she committed adultery with Cassio. Had she been true to me and had not committed adultery, I would not have traded her for a Heaven-made precious gem the size of the Earth."

"My husband?"

"Yes, he told me first about her adultery. He is an honest man, and he hates the slime that sticks on filthy deeds."

"My husband?"

"Why do you keep saying that, woman? Yes, it was your husband, Iago."

"Oh, mistress, villainy has made a mockery of your love! Was it my husband who said that she was false to you!"

"Yes, woman," Othello said. "I say that it was he, your husband, who told me that my wife was committing adultery with Cassio. Do you understand the word 'husband'? I am talking about my friend, your husband: honest, honest Iago."

"If he said that Desdemona committed adultery, may his pernicious, destructive, and evil soul rot in Hell forever! He lies entirely — all the way to his heart. Desdemona was too fond of her most filthy bargain — her marriage — to commit adultery."

"Ha!" Othello said, and he drew his sword.

"Do your worst to me," Emilia said. "This deed of yours is no more worthy of Heaven than you were worthy of her."

"Shut up, if you are wise!"

"You have not half the power to do me harm as I have the power to endure that hurt. You are a fool! You are an idiot! You are as ignorant as dirt! You have done an evil deed — I am not afraid of your sword! I will make your evil deed known to all, and I would do that even if I lost twenty lives!"

She shouted, "Help! Help! Help! The Moor has killed my mistress! Murder! Murder!"

Montano, Gratiano, and Iago entered the room.

"What is the matter?" Montano asked. "How are you now, general?"

Emilia saw her husband and said, "Oh, have you come, Iago?"

She added, sarcastically, "You have done well — men are blaming their murders on you."

Gratiano asked, "What is the matter?"

Emilia said to Iago, "Prove that Othello is lying, if you are a man. He says that you told him that his wife was false to him and had committed adultery. I know that you did not — you are not such a villain. Speak, because my heart is heavy with grief."

"I told him what I thought to be true," Iago said, "and I told him no more than what he himself found was reasonable, believable, and true."

"But did you ever tell him that Desdemona was false to him and had committed adultery?"

"I did."

"Then you told a lie — an odious, damned lie. I swear upon my soul that you told a lie, a wicked lie. Desdemona false with Cassio! Did you say that she committed adultery with Cassio?"

"With Cassio, mistress," Iago said. "Put a spell on your tongue to silence it."

"I will not be silent," Emilia said. "I must speak. My mistress, Desdemona, here lies murdered in her bed —"

Shocked, Montano and Gratiano said, "Heaven forbid!"

Emilia finished, "— and, Iago, your lying reports have caused the murder."

Montano and Gratiano stared at Othello, who said, "Do not stare, masters. What Emilia said is true, indeed. I have killed my wife."

Gratiano said, "It is a strange truth."

"It is a monstrous act!" Montano said.

"Villainy, villainy, villainy!" Emilia said. "I know it. I smell it. Oh, villainy! I suspected it previously. I'll kill myself out of grief. Oh, villainy, villainy!"

"What, are you insane?" Iago said. "I order you to go home."

"Good gentlemen, let me have leave to speak," Emilia said. "It is usually proper for me to obey my husband, but it is not proper now. Perhaps, Iago, I will never again go home."

Overcome with emotion, Othello groaned and fell on Desdemona's bed.

"Lie down there and roar with grief," Emilia said to him. "You have killed the sweetest innocent who ever lifted her eyes to Heaven as she prayed."

Othello was still unwilling to accept the truth. He stood up and said, "Desdemona was foul."

He looked at Gratiano, Desdemona's uncle, who was therefore his uncle-in-law, and said, "I scarcely did recognize you, uncle. There lies your niece, whose breath, indeed, these hands have newly stopped. I know that this act appears to be horrible and grim."

"Poor Desdemona!" Gratiano said. "I am glad that your father is dead. Your marriage to Othello was deadly to him; his grief at your marriage cut his life short — the Fates cut his thread of life. If he were still alive, this sight would make him do something desperate. He would curse his guardian angel and drive it away from his side, commit suicide, and fall into a state of damnation."

"This sight is pitiful," Othello said, "but Iago knows that she has committed adultery with Cassio a thousand times; Cassio himself confessed it, and she rewarded his amorous works with the first love-token that I gave to her. I saw it in his hand: It was a handkerchief: an antique love-token that my father gave my mother."

"Oh, Heaven!" Emilia cried. "Oh, Heavenly powers!"

"Shut up!" Iago ordered her.

"The truth will come out! The truth will come out! Will I shut up? No, I will speak as liberally as the North Wind that violently blows with bitter cold. Let Heaven and men and devils, let them all, all, all, cry shame against me because I am disobeying my husband, yet I'll speak."

"Be wise, shut up, and go home," Iago said.

"I will not."

Iago drew his sword and threatened his wife.

Gratiano was shocked: "You would draw your sword against a woman!"

"You dull Moor!" Emilia said. "By chance, I found that handkerchief you are talking about, and I gave it to my husband. Often, solemnly and earnestly, despite the handkerchief being just a trifle, he had asked me to steal it."

"You are a villainous whore!" Iago said to his wife.

"Did Desdemona give that handkerchief to Cassio? No! I found it, and I gave it to my husband."

"Filth, you lie!" Iago shouted.

"By Heaven, I do not. I do not, gentlemen," Emilia said.

She said to Othello, "Oh, murderous fool! What could such a fool as you do with so good a woman? You did not deserve her!"

Realizing that Emilia was telling the truth, Othello said, "Are there no lightning bolts in Heaven but those that are used with the thunder? Will no lightning bolts strike Iago dead?"

Othello said to Iago, "You are thoroughly a villain!"

Sword drawn, Othello ran at Iago, but Montano disarmed Othello. Iago stabbed Emilia and then fled.

Gratiano said, "Emilia has fallen. No doubt this villain has killed his wife."

"I am dying," Emilia said. "Lay me by my mistress' side."

With help from Montano and Gratiano, she staggered to the bed and lay on it.

Gratiano said, "Iago has fled, and his wife has suffered a mortal wound."

"Iago is a notorious villain," Montano said.

He said to Gratiano, "Take this weapon, which I have just taken from the Moor, and guard the door from the outside. Do not let him pass through the doorway — kill him if you have to. I will run after Iago, that damned villain — he is a damned servant of evil."

Montano and Gratiano exited the bedchamber. They thought that Emilia had died.

Othello said to himself, "I have lost my valor. Any puny whippersnapper can take my sword from me. But why should my reputation for valor outlast my valor? My reputation for honor should not outlast my honor."

Emilia said softly on the bed, "What did your song foretell, lady? Can you hear me? Swans are silent during their lives and sing only when they are dying. I will be like the swan and die as I sing."

She sang, "*Willow, willow, willow —*"

She added, "Moor, Desdemona was chaste and did not engage in immoral sex; she loved you, cruel Moor. I swear on my immortal soul that I am telling you the truth. I am telling you the truth as my soul goes to Paradise."

Those were Emilia's last words.

Othello said, "I have another weapon in this bedchamber; it is a sword of Spain, tempered in an icy brook. Here it is."

He held the sword in his hand as he called, "Uncle, I must come out of this room."

Gratiano replied, "If you attempt to leave, it will cost you dearly. You have no weapon, I do have a weapon, and therefore you will suffer."

"Come in here and talk to me," Othello said, "or, defenseless as I am, I will attack you."

Gratiano entered the room and said, "What do you want?"

Othello displayed his sword and said, "Look, I have a weapon. A better sword has never hung upon a soldier's thigh. I have seen the day that with my little arm and this good sword, I have made my way through impediments with more than twenty times your power to stop me, but I am vainly boasting. Who can control his fate? I cannot do that now. Don't be afraid, although you see me with a weapon. Here is the end of my journey — here is my stopping place and the marker that announces the farthest extent of my life."

Gratiano backed away from Othello, who asked, "Do you retreat in dismay? You are wasting your fear. Point a mere straw at Othello's chest, and I will give up. Where should Othello go?"

Othello looked at Desdemona's corpse and said, "How do you look now? Oh, ill-starred woman! You are as pale as your smock! When we shall meet on Judgment Day, this look of yours will hurl my soul from Heaven, and fiends will snatch at it and carry it away to Hell. You are cold, cold, my girl! Your chastity — your avoidance of immoral sex — lacked the heat of immoral lust. I am a cursed sinner! Whip me, devils, from the possession of this Heavenly sight! Desdemona and I will be separated in the afterlife — her abode is in Heaven, and mine is in Hell! Let hot winds blow on me! Roast me in sulfur! Wash me in precipitous chasms of liquid fire! Desdemona! Desdemona, you are dead! I have murdered you!"

Lodovico and Montano entered the room. With them was Cassio, who was being carried in a sedan chair. Officers also entered the room, leading Iago, their prisoner.

Lodovico asked, "Where is Othello, that rash and most unfortunate man?"

"The man who was Othello is here," Othello said. "I am he."

Lodovico said, "Where is that viper named Iago? Bring the villain forward."

Othello said, "I look down at Iago's feet, but he does not have cloven feet — that story about devils is a fable."

Othello said to Iago, "If you are an immortal devil, then I cannot kill you."

Othello slashed Iago with his sword.

"Wrench his sword away from him," Lodovico ordered.

Othello was disarmed.

Iago said to Othello, "I bleed, sir; but I am not killed."

"I am not sorry that you are alive," Othello said. "I prefer that you stay alive. I know now that it is happiness to die. It is better to die than to be alive."

"Othello, you were once a very good man," Lodovico said, "but you fell into the trap of this damned evil man. What can I say to you?"

"Say anything you wish," Othello said. "Call me an honorable murderer, if you will. I did nothing out of hatred; I acted only out of honorable motives."

"This wretched Iago has partly confessed his villainy," Lodovico said. "Did you and he agree to cause Cassio's death?"

"Yes," Othello replied.

Cassio said, "Respected general, I never gave you cause to wish my death."

"I believe you, and I beg you to forgive me," Othello said. "Will you, please, ask that demi-devil why he has thus ensnared my soul and body?"

"Ask me nothing," Iago said. "What you know, you know: From this time forward, I will never speak another word."

"Not even to pray?" Lodovico asked.

Gratiano said, "Torture will open your lips."

"Torture is an excellent idea," Othello said.

Lodovico said to Othello, "Sir, you shall understand what has happened. You do not, I think, know all the story. Here is a letter found in the pocket of the slain Roderigo, and here is another letter. The first letter is from Iago to Roderigo and contains information intended to help Roderigo kill Cassio."

"Iago is a villain," Othello said.

Cassio said, "This attempted murder is very heathenish and very gross!"

"Here is another letter that we found in Roderigo's pocket," Lodovico said. "It seems that Roderigo meant to send this letter of complaint to Iago but Iago met with Roderigo just before he sent the letter; Iago answered his complaints."

"Iago is a pernicious caitiff!" Othello said. "He is a malignant and contemptible person!"

He added, "Cassio, how did you come to possess that handkerchief that belonged to my wife?"

"I found it in my bedchamber," Cassio replied. "Iago himself confessed just now that he dropped it there as part of his plan to ruin you."

"I have been a fool!" Othello said. "A fool! A fool!"

Cassio said, "Roderigo's letter in which he upbraids Iago contains more information. Roderigo wrote that Iago made him attack me while I was on guard duty, resulting in my dismissal as Othello's lieutenant. Just now Roderigo gave us more information. We thought that he had been dead a long time, but he revived briefly before dying for real and told us that Iago had wounded him and that previously Iago had urged him to try to murder me."

Lodovico said to Othello, "You must leave this room, and go with us. Your power and your command are removed from you; Cassio now rules in Cyprus. As for this villain, Iago, if there exists any cunning cruelty that can torment him greatly without killing him for a long time, he will feel that torture. You, Othello, will be our prisoner until we inform the Venetian government about the nature of your fault. The Venetian government will decide what shall be done with you."

He said to the guards in the bedchamber, "Come, take the Moor away."

Othello said, "Wait. Let me say a word or two before you go. I have done the Venetian government some service, and they know it, but no more of that. Please, in your letters, when you shall relate these unlucky deeds, speak of me as I am. Make no excuses for me, and do not write anything out of malice. You must write about me as one who loved not wisely but too well — I should have loved moderately but instead I loved excessively. You must write about me as one who was not easily jealous, but as one who was manipulated into being extremely jealous. You must write about me as one whose hand, like the hand of a lowly ranking man of India, threw a pearl away that was more valuable than all his tribe. You must write about me as one whose eyes, although unaccustomed to crying, dropped tears when overcome with grief as quickly as Arabian trees drop the medicinal myrrh that oozes from them. Write all this down, and add that in Aleppo once, where a malignant and evil turbaned Turkish Muslim beat a Venetian man and slandered the Venetian state, I took the circumcised Muslim dog by the throat and killed him although it was a capital crime for a Christian — and I am a Christian — to strike a Turk."

Othello was a military man, and military men often keep weapons hidden on their bodies. Othello took out a hidden dagger and said, "I killed the Turk like this" — then he stabbed himself mortally.

Lodovico said, "This is a bloody conclusion to Othello's life!"

"All that we planned to do concerning Othello is ruined," Gratiano said. "It is no longer applicable."

Othello said to Desdemona's corpse, "I kissed you before I killed you. There is nothing left to do but this — having killed myself, to die with a kiss."

He fell on the bed, kissed Desdemona's corpse, and died.

"I was afraid that Othello might try to kill himself," Cassio said, "but I thought he had no weapon. Othello was great of heart."

Lodovico said to Iago, "You vicious Spartan dog — deadlier than anguish, hunger, or the sea! — look at the tragic corpses on this bed. This is your doing. This spectacle poisons men's sight."

He ordered, "Draw the bed curtains and let the corpses be hidden from sight."

He then said, "Gratiano, stay in the house, and take legal possession of the belongings and money of the Moor. You are the next of kin, and you inherit his fortune."

He said to Cassio, "To you, lord governor, falls the punishment of Iago, this Hellish villain; you decide the time, the place, the torture — enforce justice!"

He concluded, "I myself will immediately return to Venice, and to the Venetian state, I will these sad events with heavy heart relate."

APPENDIX A: ABOUT THE AUTHOR

It was a dark and stormy night. Suddenly a cry rang out, and on a hot summer night in 1954, Josephine, wife of Carl Bruce, gave birth to a boy — me. Unfortunately, this young married couple allowed Reuben Saturday, Josephine's brother, to name their first-born. Reuben, aka "The Joker," decided that Bruce was a nice name, so he decided to name me Bruce Bruce. I have gone by my middle name — David — ever since.

Being named Bruce David Bruce hasn't been all bad. Bank tellers remember me very quickly, so I don't often have to show an ID. It can be fun in charades, also. When I was a counselor as a teenager at Camp Echoing Hills in Warsaw, Ohio, a fellow counselor gave the signs for "sounds like" and "two words," then she pointed to a bruise on her leg twice. Bruise Bruise? Oh yeah, Bruce Bruce is the answer!

Uncle Reuben, by the way, gave me a haircut when I was in kindergarten. He cut my hair short and shaved a small bald spot on the back of my head. My mother wouldn't let me go to school until the bald spot grew out again.

Of all my brothers and sisters (six in all), I am the only transplant to Athens, Ohio. I was born in Newark, Ohio, and have lived all around Southeastern Ohio. However, I moved to Athens to go to Ohio University and have never left.

At Ohio U, I never could make up my mind whether to major in English or Philosophy, so I got a bachelor's degree with a double major in both areas, then I added a Master of Arts degree in English and a Master of Arts degree in Philosophy. Yes, I have my MAMA degree.

Currently, and for a long time to come (I eat fruits and vegetables), I am spending my retirement writing books such as *Nadia Comaneci: Perfect 10*, *The Funniest People in Dance*, *Homer's* Iliad: *A Retelling in Prose*, and *William Shakespeare's* King Lear: *A Retelling in Prose*.

By the way, my sister Brenda Kennedy writes romances such as *A New Beginning* and *Shattered Dreams*.

APPENDIX B: SOME BOOKS BY DAVID BRUCE

Retellings of a Classic Work of Literature

Arden of Faversham: *A Retelling*

Ben Jonson's The Alchemist: *A Retelling*

Ben Jonson's The Arraignment, or Poetaster: *A Retelling*

Ben Jonson's Bartholomew Fair: *A Retelling*

Ben Jonson's The Case is Altered: *A Retelling*

Ben Jonson's Catiline's Conspiracy: *A Retelling*

Ben Jonson's The Devil is an Ass: *A Retelling*

Ben Jonson's Epicene: *A Retelling*

Ben Jonson's Every Man in His Humor: *A Retelling*

Ben Jonson's Every Man Out of His Humor: *A Retelling*

Ben Jonson's The Fountain of Self-Love, or Cynthia's Revels: *A Retelling*

Ben Jonson's The Magnetic Lady, or Humors Reconciled: *A Retelling*

Ben Jonson's The New Inn, or The Light Heart: *A Retelling*

Ben Jonson's Sejanus' Fall: *A Retelling*

Ben Jonson's The Staple of News: *A Retelling*

Ben Jonson's A Tale of a Tub: *A Retelling*

Ben Jonson's Volpone, or the Fox: *A Retelling*

Christopher Marlowe's Complete Plays: Retellings

Christopher Marlowe's Dido, Queen of Carthage: *A Retelling*

Christopher Marlowe's Doctor Faustus: *Retellings of the 1604 A-Text and of the 1616 B-Text*

Christopher Marlowe's Edward II: *A Retelling*

Christopher Marlowe's The Massacre at Paris: *A Retelling*

Christopher Marlowe's The Rich Jew of Malta: *A Retelling*

Christopher Marlowe's Tamburlaine, Parts 1 and 2: *Retellings*

Dante's Divine Comedy: *A Retelling in Prose*

Dante's Inferno: *A Retelling in Prose*

Dante's Purgatory: *A Retelling in Prose*

Dante's Paradise: *A Retelling in Prose*

The Famous Victories of Henry V: *A Retelling*

From the Iliad *to the* Odyssey: *A Retelling in Prose of Quintus of Smyrna's* Posthomerica

George Chapman, Ben Jonson, and John Marston's Eastward Ho! *A Retelling*

George Peele's The Arraignment of Paris: *A Retelling*

George Peele's The Battle of Alcazar: *A Retelling*

George's Peele's David and Bathsheba, and the Tragedy of Absalom: *A Retelling*

George Peele's Edward I: *A Retelling*

George Peele's The Old Wives' Tale: *A Retelling*

George-a-Greene: *A Retelling*

The History of King Leir: *A Retelling*

Homer's Iliad: *A Retelling in Prose*

Homer's Odyssey: *A Retelling in Prose*

J.W. Gent.'s The Valiant Scot: *A Retelling*

Jason and the Argonauts: A Retelling in Prose of Apollonius of Rhodes' Argonautica

John Ford: Eight Plays Translated into Modern English

John Ford's The Broken Heart: *A Retelling*

John Ford's The Fancies, Chaste and Noble: *A Retelling*

John Ford's The Lady's Trial: *A Retelling*

John Ford's The Lover's Melancholy: *A Retelling*

John Ford's Love's Sacrifice: *A Retelling*

John Ford's Perkin Warbeck: *A Retelling*

John Ford's The Queen: *A Retelling*

John Ford's 'Tis Pity She's a Whore: *A Retelling*

John Lyly's Campaspe: *A Retelling*

John Lyly's Endymion, The Man in the Moon: *A Retelling*

John Lyly's Galatea: *A Retelling*

John Lyly's Love's Metamorphosis: *A Retelling*

John Lyly's Midas: *A Retelling*

John Lyly's Mother Bombie: *A Retelling*

John Lyly's Sappho and Phao: *A Retelling*

John Lyly's The Woman in the Moon: *A Retelling*

John Webster's The White Devil: *A Retelling*

King Edward III: *A Retelling*

Mankind: *A Medieval Morality Play* (A Retelling)

Margaret Cavendish's The Unnatural Tragedy: *A Retelling*

The Merry Devil of Edmonton: *A Retelling*

The Summoning of Everyman: *A Medieval Morality Play* (A Retelling)

Robert Greene's Friar Bacon and Friar Bungay: *A Retelling*

The Taming of a Shrew: *A Retelling*

Tarlton's Jests: A Retelling

Thomas Middleton's A Chaste Maid in Cheapside: *A Retelling*

Thomas Middleton's Women Beware Women: *A Retelling*

Thomas Middleton and Thomas Dekker's The Roaring Girl: *A Retelling*

Thomas Middleton and William Rowley's The Changeling: *A Retelling*

The Trojan War and Its Aftermath: Four Ancient Epic Poems

Virgil's Aeneid: *A Retelling in Prose*

William Shakespeare's 5 Late Romances: Retellings in Prose

William Shakespeare's 10 Histories: Retellings in Prose

William Shakespeare's 11 Tragedies: Retellings in Prose

William Shakespeare's 12 Comedies: Retellings in Prose

William Shakespeare's 38 Plays: Retellings in Prose

William Shakespeare's 1 Henry IV, aka Henry IV, Part 1: A Retelling in Prose

William Shakespeare's 2 Henry IV, aka Henry IV, Part 2: A Retelling in Prose

William Shakespeare's 1 Henry VI, aka Henry VI, Part 1: A Retelling in Prose

William Shakespeare's 2 Henry VI, aka Henry VI, Part 2: A Retelling in Prose

William Shakespeare's 3 Henry VI, aka Henry VI, Part 3: A Retelling in Prose

William Shakespeare's All's Well that Ends Well: A Retelling in Prose

William Shakespeare's Antony and Cleopatra: A Retelling in Prose

William Shakespeare's As You Like It: A Retelling in Prose

William Shakespeare's The Comedy of Errors: A Retelling in Prose

William Shakespeare's Coriolanus: A Retelling in Prose

William Shakespeare's Cymbeline: A Retelling in Prose

William Shakespeare's Hamlet: A Retelling in Prose

William Shakespeare's Henry V: A Retelling in Prose

William Shakespeare's Henry VIII: A Retelling in Prose

William Shakespeare's Julius Caesar: A Retelling in Prose

William Shakespeare's King John: A Retelling in Prose

William Shakespeare's King Lear: A Retelling in Prose

William Shakespeare's Love's Labor's Lost: A Retelling in Prose

William Shakespeare's Macbeth: A Retelling in Prose

William Shakespeare's Measure for Measure: A Retelling in Prose

William Shakespeare's The Merchant of Venice: A Retelling in Prose

William Shakespeare's The Merry Wives of Windsor: A Retelling in Prose

William Shakespeare's A Midsummer Night's Dream: A Retelling in Prose

William Shakespeare's Much Ado About Nothing: A Retelling in Prose

William Shakespeare's Othello: A Retelling in Prose

William Shakespeare's Pericles, Prince of Tyre: A Retelling in Prose

William Shakespeare's Richard II: A Retelling in Prose

William Shakespeare's Richard III: A Retelling in Prose

William Shakespeare's Romeo and Juliet: A Retelling in Prose

William Shakespeare's The Taming of the Shrew: A Retelling in Prose

William Shakespeare's The Tempest: A Retelling in Prose

William Shakespeare's Timon of Athens: A Retelling in Prose

William Shakespeare's Titus Andronicus: A Retelling in Prose

William Shakespeare's Troilus and Cressida: A Retelling in Prose

William Shakespeare's Twelfth Night: A Retelling in Prose

William Shakespeare's The Two Gentlemen of Verona: A Retelling in Prose

William Shakespeare's The Two Noble Kinsmen: A Retelling in Prose

William Shakespeare's The Winter's Tale: A Retelling in Prose

9 7 9 8 2 0 1 4 6 9 2 3 8